SASKIA

CW00859095

UNLEASHED
An anthology of erotic fiction

by
Saskia Walker

UNLEASHED
© Saskia Walker

This collection was first published in 2010
This edition published 2014

This is a work of fiction. Names, characters, places and incidents are solely the product of the author's imagination and/or are used fictitiously, though reference may be made to actual historical events or existing locations. Any resemblance to actual persons, living or dead, business establishments, events or locales is entirely coincidental.

This book is not transferable. It is for your own personal use. If it is sold, shared, or given away, it is an infringement of the copyright of this work.

Please note: this book is for sale to adults only. It contains sexually explicit scenes and graphic language which may be considered offensive by some readers.

Cover design: Frauke Spanuth at Croco Designs.
Photo Credit: Mayer George

UNLEASHED

Table of Contents	**Page**

Room with a View	5
Watching Lois Perform	13
Sign Your Name	25
Richard's Secret	35
Hungry for Love	47
The Lunch Break	51
The Importance of Good Networking	63
Keeping Time	75
The Woman in His Room	81
A Hook and a Twist	93
The Upper Hand	103
Counting the Days	115
The Inner Vixen	127
Live Tonight	137
The Things That Go On At Siesta Time	149
It's Just Not Cricket	159
Harvest Time	171
Rapt	181
Caught Watching	193
Winter Heat	199
Credits	209
About the Author	211

The stories in this collection are sexual fantasies.
Please practice safe sex in real life.

SASKIA WALKER

ROOM WITH A VIEW

Fiona took a gulp of her wine and put her glass down, pushing it across the rough, wooden table with a sigh. "Damn it. I am so horny." She glanced around the small village bar with a resigned expression. "And not a hint of action for miles."

I gave a wry smile. "Hiking through Brittany was meant to be good for our souls, but you're right, maybe we should have gone to Paris instead, especially if you're on a manhunt." I was teasing her. I knew Fiona couldn't go for long without a tumble. I had to admit all this fresh air and plodding was also making me crave exercise of a much more stimulating and intimate kind.

"I thought we might meet a fit and eager young farmhand who wanted a roll in the hay." She looked positively woebegone, her pretty mouth down-turned, her brown eyes sad.

I laughed. "You're just bored." I glanced over at the barman, or "*grand-pere*" as he was called by the handful of occupants. It was a very small village. "*Grand-pere* over there might be able to help you out."

"I'm not that desperate. Yet." She laughed, and then she glanced at the door behind me, her eyes rounding. I heard it creak open. Someone else had arrived. I watched her face for her reaction.

Her expression lit up. She leaned forward and put her elbows on the table, ruffling her fingers through her shoulder-length, curly blonde hair to restore life to it. "Oh, my prayers have been answered, a man has appeared."

I glanced around casually, brushing an imaginary piece of fluff off my shoulder. Given Fi's reaction, I was half expecting to see a bronzed god standing in the doorway. Not quite, but he was definitely worth a once-over, sexy in a sort of sleazy way-wide, cheesy grin, slicked-back hair and figure-hugging clothes. A pair of sunglasses hung from the neckline of his designer T-shirt. A stud, and most definitely a fellow tourist. I turned back. "He put a smile on your face."

"Mmm," she purred. "Now that's what I'm talking about." Just as she said it, her face fell. "Oh damn, he's got a woman with him, she's just come in behind him."

I couldn't stop myself from glancing back. The woman was scanning the bar and its occupants with a disapproving look. She was tall and glamorous-way too glamorous for this place-and looked as if she was afraid she might catch something if she sat down in here. She tucked her burgundy-dyed bob behind her ears and stepped forward on her slender heels, as if walking out onto a catwalk. An amused murmur went round the locals.

Fiona rolled her eyes. "She's gorgeous. I hate her."

"At least the locals didn't laugh at us," I commented, suddenly proud that we had been more easily accepted.

Everyone watched as the couple walked to the bar. There didn't seem to be any pressing need to turn away. Fiona sighed deeply. She was looking at the guy's tight derriere as he leaned over the bar to give his order. "I'd like to see that butt naked."

"You're making it worse on yourself," I murmured, imagining him naked too. His arsecheeks were taut, flexing inside the tight denim of his jeans. Beneath his T-shirt, the muscles of his back were subtly defined.

I turned back to Fiona when the couple picked up a carafe of wine and looked for somewhere to sit. Apart from the row of five stools at the bar-all full with locals-there were only three small tables in the place. They took the table just a few feet away from us. The woman glanced over but never acknowledged us. The guy grinned. Fiona grinned back. I smiled and nodded. The couple spoke to each other in French. Briefly. As soon as they got settled, he started kissing the woman's neck, his hands moving all over her.

"That lucky bitch, she's going to get shagged tonight," Fiona whispered under her breath.

"I agree, but that's not the worst part. Unless they're relatives of *grand-pere* and his brood, which I very much doubt since they got the same dour greeting we did, they must be staying at the *gite* with us." The farmhouse bed and breakfast had three guest rooms. Marie, the owner, had told us she was expecting another party. The hands-on couple had to be the other guests.

"Oh great, I get to look at that over breakfast too." She nodded over at them. The stud had his hand under the woman's short skirt and was stroking her thigh. The woman sipped her wine, her face expressionless. "What an ice queen," Fiona added, chuckling into her drink.

What a waste, I thought, and waved at *grand-pere* for another carafe of wine.

The guest rooms were located in a teetering barn, converted to provide sparse but pretty accommodation. We made it back to our attic room, up a rickety staircase that had us breathless and giggling by the time we reached the top. We were high on oxygen, wine and sexual need.

The two hard, narrow beds looked much more inviting than they did before we'd had the wine. Fiona threw herself onto the nearest one, unzipping her jeans and fighting them and her boots off as she did so. "Oh, if he were single and here right now?"

"What would you do with him?"

"First, I'd make him lick my breasts, every inch." She grabbed her breasts through her T-shirt, massaging them deeply.

I kicked my walking boots off, shucking my T-shirt over my head.

7

Fiona was still lost in her fantasy. "Then I'd make him go down." She thrust her hand inside her undies. A raised knuckle poking up through the soft fabric indicated that she'd headed straight for her clit.

"This isn't helping." I laughed.

"You're right," she replied, tugging her hand free. She pulled her T-shirt and undies off, clambering under the sheets with a deep sigh.

We were just getting settled down and I was about to turn off the light when we heard a door shut, footsteps, and the creaking of the staircase. Voices sounded in the room below. Then it started-loud, ecstatic moaning-the sounds of a woman in extreme pleasure.

Fiona half sat and stared across at me, her expression incredulous. "Bloody hell, the ice queen had to be a moaner, didn't she?"

I shook my head. "It's adding insult to injury."

Fiona shut her eyes, pressing her head back into her pillow.

"*Oh oui! Vite, vite,*" the voice from below shouted.

"That lucky bitch," Fiona groaned, her hand moving under her sheet, reaching between her restless thighs.

She began rubbing and heat spread through my body, part embarrassment and part red-hot arousal. "Jesus, Fi. If you have to masturbate can't you at least turn the light out first?" What with the sound effects from below, and her obvious actions, I was fast growing wet. I squeezed my thighs together. My clit felt as if it was wired to a jagged electric current, my inner flesh aching for contact. I reached for the cord and clicked off the light. I dropped back on my pillows, wishing away the lust that had taken hold of me. As I did, I became aware of a shaft of eerie light, spanning from floor to ceiling. "What the hell is that?" I sat bolt upright, clutching the sheet to my chest, thoroughly spooked.

Fi was already out of bed and tiptoeing across the floor, her naked body strangely lit by the shaft of light. "It must be a hole in the floorboards." She knelt down, blocking out the light as she moved over it. "Oh my god," she hissed, drawing back. The light beamed upward again. "Get over here. It's a knot in the wood that's fallen out. We're right over their bed and he's giving her one hell of a pussy licking."

That did it. My hormones were already in overdrive and now they were spilling over. As I stood up, moisture ran onto my inner thighs. I clamped them shut, wriggling them together, nearly falling over as I did so. She'd all but blocked out the light, hovering over it, but I made it over to the spot and dropped to my knees beside her. She pulled back and pointed at it, one hand covering her mouth as if she was afraid she might laugh.

I peered through the hole, gasping with amazement when I caught sight of them. The ice queen was on her back, naked, her breasts jutting outward as she lay spread-eagled on the bed. Her dark nipples and red bob looked strange and vivid against her pale flesh and the white sheets. The stud was working away in between her legs, his head bobbing and his back flexing. His bare buttocks were clenching and unclenching.

"What's happening?" Fiona pushed me aside. "Oh my god. He's humping the edge of the bed."

"Shush, they'll hear you."

"What, with that din going on?"

"*Encore*," the ice queen bellowed, panting loudly.

Fi sat back on her haunches, one hand over her mouth, giggling. The light from the upward beam lit her face. Her eyes were full of mischief. "It looks like he's about to come all over the end of the bed."

I angled in for another glimpse. She was right. He was giving the bed some serious hip thrusts with his lower body, while seeing to the woman with his hands and mouth.

Fiona was busy moving around to my right-hand side. "Look."

I glanced up. She'd pulled back the rug at the foot of her bed and revealed another shaft of light.

"You stay there," she said. "I can't see much of her, but I've got more of him over here."

That suited me fine. I liked watching her expression changing while he did the business. Besides, the way Fi was so practical and matter-of-fact about playing peeping tom made me want to laugh aloud. I felt so naughty. Combined with the heady flow of lust in my veins, it was doing dangerous things to me. Furtively, I pushed my hand over my mons and fingered my swollen clit. Downstairs, the ice queen was rapidly melting. Her mouth was open, her body shuddering visibly as she shifted and arched. A great juddering moan left her lips, outdoing all her previous exhortations for pitch and reverberation. The stud moved, standing, murmuring encouragement to her in a low voice. For the first time I got a glimpse of his cock, and what an eyeful it was.

"Bloody hell," Fi whispered across the floor.

"I know," I hissed back, watching as he stroked it with a sure and adoring fist.

The ice queen sat up and smiled at him. It was the first time I'd seen her smile. She rolled closer to the edge of the bed and onto her hands and knees, her bottom wiggling in the air as she lowered her head to his groin. On her lower back, she had a tribal tattoo, a dark shape etched beneath her pale skin. When she started to mouth his cock, his head dropped back and his eyes shut, his slicked-back hair finally falling free of his skull to drop to one side.

The ice queen seemed able to make a lot of noise at all times-even with her mouth full. She concentrated her actions on his cock head, tonguing it and taking it into her

10

mouth as if that was all that would fit. Mind you, it was very large.

"Oh come on. I'd give you a much better blow job than that, big boy," Fiona said, laughing to herself. "Suck it in, ice queen."

"No, if she did that we'd get to see less of it."

"True. Hey, ice queen, don't suck it in, we wanna see it."

"Fiona!" She was drunk. So was I, but she was verging on blowing our cover.

"Oops." She put her hand over her mouth again, leaning back from her peephole and resting on her knees to quell her laughter. The beam of light showed her ample breasts bouncing as she moved. The triangle of dark blonde hair in her groin was just visible in the fall of light. Her body was outlined with darkness, her pubic hair glistening. Everywhere I looked I saw flesh and sexually alert people. And I was no exception. My nether regions were trembling with need, my hips swiveling of their own accord, ready and primed for action. Fi's hand shot to her pussy, rubbing fast as she ducked back down to look again.

What had started out as a red-hot, full-on sex show had now developed into a double-trouble, split-screen project. Overwhelmed with stimulation, I glanced from the shadowy image of Fiona masturbating and back to the scene below. My hand was now buried between my thighs, one finger shoved inside and the heel of my hand over my clit, crushing it. I was going to come at any moment.

Downstairs, the stud was wanking his shaft while the woman sucked on the head of his cock. He'd reached one hand lower, presumably to hold his balls. How I wished I could see that too. The ice queen pulled back suddenly and knelt up, walking on her knees right up against him, whispering, gesturing at his cock then squeezing her breasts in her hands. The stud wanked faster

11

as he looked at her tits, his cock-end dark with blood and glistening wet, his moving hand aiming it right at her.

I trembled, my climax building and rolling from my center. My sex clenched, spasmed, and flooded. Hot waves of pleasure shot through my entire groin. I wavered, slid, thought I'd slip flat out and right across the floor. The hand pivoting me on the floor was damp and I fumbled for steadiness. I blinked, attempted to ground myself, and refocused on the view below, not wanting to miss the sight of him coming.

Seconds later, he let rip and shot his load, thick white ribbons of semen covering the space between them. The hand between my thighs was drenched. Just a couple of feet away, I could hear Fi sighing with pleasure.

"Jesus, that was hot," I managed to whisper to her a moment later, suddenly self-conscious about what we'd done. I'd lost it, the intensity of the moment compelling me to watch, to enjoy and to come.

Fiona had stood up and was staggering back to her bed, feeling her way. She gave a breathy laugh. "Yeah, and if they're staying another night, I suggest we do too. You've got to admit, it's the best fun we've had so far on this bloody trip."

I shook my head: she was so right. "You know, Fi, that's the best idea I've heard all week."

WATCHING LOIS PERFORM

"Trust me, Lois." Jack's arm shot out, blocking the doorway to her office. "I know what you need." His shirt sleeve was rolled up, revealing a strong forearm dusted with black hair, his fist sure and large against the door frame.

Halted in her steps, Lois took a deep breath. Her glance moved to meet his. "Trust me, Jack, you don't." Steeling herself, she pushed his arm aside, ignoring his knowing look, ignoring those dark eyes filled with suggestion and the tangible wall of testosterone he exuded.

She headed for her desk, her stiletto heels clicking on the floor. The skin on her back prickled with awareness, awareness brought about by his presence. He'd done it again. He'd made her curious, responsive. Lois didn't take any nonsense from the men she worked with, but Jack Fulton had unsettled her. Counting to five, she put her laptop down on the desk and turned to face him, ready to challenge his comment. The door was ajar, the space empty. He was gone.

She shook her head. "Typical." Grabbing her bag and coat, she left the building.

The pavement outside was growing crowded with commuters; the Friday evening London rush hour was under way. She stepped into the crush, leaving the office behind, hurrying to the tube station and descending the escalator at a pace. The display board told her it was four minutes until her train was due. She strode up and down the platform, her body wired. She was always like this after delivering a successful presentation. It had gone well, and she'd easily dealt with the put-downs issued by the men who defied her female power. She thrived on her success, but now she longed to throw off her city suit and heels.

The crowd thickened on the platform behind her, noisy and restless. Wind funneled down the tunnel, a distant train rumbled. She glanced across the tracks. Her breath caught in her throat when she saw Jack standing opposite her, still as a predator about to pounce. A barely perceptible smile lifted the corners of his mouth. Even across the rail tracks she could see the intense look in his eyes.

She swallowed. What was it about Jack Fulton? The way he looked at her did powerful things to her, sexual things. They'd worked together for just a few months, but he was one of the few men who didn't challenge her. Instead he sat back with a secret smile, watching as she defended herself at board meetings, where she proved over and again that she had earned her right to be in this male dominated world. But it was more than that. His dark sexuality was evident in the way he carried himself and the way he scrutinized her. He made her self-aware in the extreme, her underwear soon growing damp when his gaze followed her with that knowing look in his eyes. *The knowing look he had on right now.*

He inclined his head in greeting. She nodded back and then glanced away, fidgeting with the strap of her shoulder bag. One minute until her train would arrive. His earlier comment echoed through her mind. *I know what you need.* Her curiosity was growing. Her instant denial had been because of the controversy at the meeting, where she'd been giving the research stats for a proposal to change the power source in the company's major manufacturing plant. Men were always telling her they knew better than her, even though it was her field of expertise. As soon as she'd rebuffed Jack's comment about knowing what she needed, she'd realized he meant something other than work. Something more intimate. She wanted to know more. And he'd gone.

Glancing back, she saw that his train was approaching. He never took his eyes off her. She craned her neck when her view was obscured by the moving carriages. The shift of the crowd into the train made it impossible to pick him out. Then it was gone. The platform was empty. She stared at the place where he had stood until her train pulled in. She moved to the far side of the carriage, where she could stand out her journey, and turned on her heel-just in time to see Jack close in behind her.

"Your place it is then." His eyes glittered with anticipation, with certainty.

Her heart thudded in her chest. Her lips parted, but this time no retort emerged. Between her thighs, a pulse throbbed with need. She closed her mouth, snatching at the overhead handhold for support.

His smile was triumphant.

Later, in her flat, he threw her by rejecting a comfortable, relaxed seat on the sofa. Instead he pulled out a dining chair, indicating that she do the same and sit facing him.

He'd teased her all the way home, innuendo in his every word, keeping her wired. And now, despite the fact they were in her home, he took charge immediately. Not in an aggressive way, but with a relaxed sense of surety that was disarming. She put her wineglass down on the table and took her seat, noting how exposed the set up made her feel.

He lounged back over his chair, one leg folded, his ankle resting on the opposite knee, his hand loosely on the juncture. His looks were rugged but suave. He was dangerously attractive.

She tried to look as relaxed as he was, but she was far from it.

"I enjoyed watching you deal with that moron Laybourne at today's meeting."

She gave a breathy laugh, releasing some of the tension he had aroused in her. "He's just an arrogant little prick with very little real knowledge."

"You're so right." He gave a deep and genuine laugh. "He's jealous of your abilities though, and he's lusting after your body. The two vying motivations confuse him. Lust for a competitor can screw with a guy's mind." He looked at her with deliberation.

Her heart raced. "It can?"

"If he lets it." His gaze moved over her body, slowly.

"And are you jealous of my skills?" She crossed her legs, crushing the pounding pulse in her clit.

"No, I admire them immensely. I'm not threatened by you."

For a moment silence hung heavy in the atmosphere.

He raised one eyebrow. "I notice you didn't ask if I lusted after you."

"I don't think you came here with the sole purpose of analyzing today's meeting."

He tipped his glass at her. "Indeed. And you did let me come home with you."

She couldn't deny it. "So I did."

Silent acknowledgement raced between them. They were going to fuck.

He took a sip of his wine, eyeing her as she crossed and uncrossed her legs.

"It's not easy for you, is it? Blonde, pretty, extraordinarily intelligent."

16

Something akin to relief hit her. "No, it isn't." She smiled, genuinely appreciating his words. He really had been observing her.

"What do you usually do, when you bring a man home for sex?" He said it as if he was discussing the weather, and glanced around the open-plan living area, as if the furniture could tell tales.

"Oh, fast, dirty sex, nothing prolonged in terms of involvement. I don't have time." She pushed her heavy hair back from her face, watching for his response. It was the truth. What would he think of her?

"That doesn't surprise me."

"Really?"

"Perhaps you should make time."

"Perhaps I should." *Where was he going with this*?

"How many times do you reach orgasm, when you have 'fast, dirty sex'?"

It felt as if the temperature had risen dramatically. "That's a rather intimate question."

"I mean to be intimate with you, Lois."

He wasn't kidding. His provocative questioning had her entire skin prickling. "Once, mostly," she replied eventually.

He nodded. "I'd like to see you come more than once. You deserve better than that."

If he'd wanted to grab her attention, he'd certainly found the way. Up until that moment she could have turned away, asked him to leave. Not now. Not anymore.

"There's a determination about you that fascinates me," he continued. "You stalk after everything. If we were living in a primitive world, you would be a powerful huntress."

She smiled at the image, loving it. "Very amusing, but what's your point?"

"My point is that even powerful women can learn by pacing themselves. " He ran one finger around the rim of his wineglass. "You might benefit from restraint."

Her sex clenched. The nape of her neck felt damp. "You're suggesting bondage?" She let her gaze wander over his body. Bulky with muscle, his expensive clothing barely concealed his obvious strength. Being under him would be quite something.

He shook his head. "No. I'm talking about a different kind of restraint altogether. Willpower. I enjoy seeing you battle with your energies, using and controlling your power in the workplace. Whether it's in the boardroom or elsewhere, your desires are only just harnessed. You're a powerful woman, but it's as if you're always on the edge of losing control. And that is such a turn on."

Breathing had become difficult. More than that, his words about willpower struck a note with her, as if she recognized herself in what he said. She never thought about it that way, but yes. He was right.

He smiled and it was filled with dangerous charm. "I'm enjoying watching you now; you're racked with sexual tension. I can almost touch it." He moved his hand, as if he was touching her through the atmosphere. "Your eyes are dilated, slightly glazed. Your body is restless, your movements self conscious, jumpy, your skin is flushed. Your nipples are hard."

She took a gulp of wine. The way he described her was sending her cunt into overdrive.

He loosened his tie. "You've been squirming on that seat for the last five minutes. I'd put money on your underwear being very, very damp."

Her skin raced with sensation, the thrill of his words touching her every inch of skin, inside and out. She wanted to fuck. Now. But he was making her sit there and listen, controlling her with his intimate, knowing words.

18

His glance dropped to her cleavage. She realized her fingers were toying with the button there. She clutched it tight, stilling her hand, and bit her lip.

"Be careful, you'll draw blood."

He didn't miss a thing.

"How wet are you, Lois?"

She squirmed on her chair, desperate for contact, her eyes closing as she replied. "Wet, very wet." She stifled a whimper.

Silence hung heavy between them again while she looked at him for his response. He was still as a bird of prey, his chin resting on one hand. A large bulge showed in his expensive Armani pants. She wanted it badly, wanted it inside her where her body was begging to be filled.

He lifted one finger, gesturing at her crotch. "Open your legs, show me."

Swearing under her breath, she followed his instruction, wriggling her short skirt up and over her hips, her eyes never leaving his. As she opened her legs, pivoting out on her stacked heels, his eyes darkened.

"Oh yes, you are wet." His lips remained apart as he stared at her. She sensed his breathing had grown quicker. "Touch yourself, through your panties."

She rested her hand over her pussy and groaned aloud. Her clit leapt, her hips wriggling into her hand for more.

"Enough." He smiled. "Stand and take your underwear off."

Her heart thudded so hard she thought she might crack. She took a deep breath and stood up, rested her thumbs in the lacy waist band and paused.

With one finger, he gestured downwards.

She rolled them over her hipbones, growling quietly when she found herself exposed under his gaze. Dropping the panties to the floor, she stepped out of them. Her skirt was wedged around her waist, her pussy

19

exposed. She rested her hands on her hips in an attempt to feel less awkward.

"How delicious. I can see your clit poking out. It's very swollen, isn't it?"

She nodded, her feet shuffling, her face on fire.

He gestured at her abandoned panties. "Pick them up and bring them here."

His instruction hit her like a left hook. He wanted her damp underwear. She steadied herself. Bending to snatch them up, she looked at the floor, counted to five. He also wanted her to move closer. Standing up, barely in touch with her equilibrium, she swayed on her heels. When she stepped forward, she had the panties clutched against her chest.

He gestured with his hand.

She held them out.

He leaned forward, took the wispy garment. Slowly, he opened the crotch out, holding it up to the light. "Poor Lois, you were finding this hard, weren't you?" A damp patch reminiscent of a Rorschach print spanned the entire fabric. He breathed in appreciatively, his eyelids lowering. "Delicious."

A combination of embarrassment and nagging lust burned her up inside. Her juices were now marking the insides of her thighs. "Do you get off on making women hot," she blurted, "and then leaving them hanging?"

He rested the panties on the table, next to his wineglass, and put his hand over the bulge in his pants. "I'm a slave to this as much as you are."

"Hardly." He was so controlled. She felt as if she was about to lose it and beg. Was that what he wanted her to do?

He moved his hand, unzipping his pants and letting his cock spring free. Moisture dribbled from its tip. With one hand, he rode it up and down, slowly and deliberately, watching her reaction. It was long and thick, a prize specimen, and it was as ready for action as she was. When she glanced back up at his face, she saw it all, saw a mirror of where she was at, wrestling with her inner desires, barely controlling them.

"Hard, isn't it?" His mouth moved in an ironic smile.

"Please. Jack, please?" Her hand had found its way into her pussy.

He watched her hand moving. "What is it that you want?"

"That." She nodded down at his cock, her hand latched over her clit, pressing and squeezing. "Inside me."

"Show me how much you want it."

She stared at him, panting with need, then instinct took over and she dropped to a crouch, moving to kneel at his feet. She opened her shirt, pulled the cups of her bra down so that her tits pushed out. She plucked at her rigid nipples. "I want it so much," she whispered, looking up at him pleadingly. She licked his cock with her tongue, from where his fist was braced around its base, up to the tip and over.

His eyes gleamed with pleasure, his lips parted.

She took the swollen head into her mouth, riding it against the roof of her mouth. When he groaned, she took him deeper, rising and falling, sucking him hard. His hand loosened, his balls rode high. She drew back.

He looked down at her, his eyes glazed. Still he made no move. Her hips swung behind her, her arse in the air, her cunt begging to be filled. "Please, please fuck me. Jack, I'm dying for you to fuck me."

It was as if she'd tripped a switch with those words.

Undoing his belt, he stood up, shoving his pants and jockeys to his ankles. He hauled her to her feet, kissed her fiercely, his tongue claiming her lips, her mouth. Between them, one hand moved on his cock, the other stroked her pussy, squeezing it in his hand, sending her clit wild. She whimpered, entirely locked to his actions.

He grabbed her by the shoulders and turned her round, bending her over the dining table, pressing her down onto it, his hands roaming over her exposed buttocks as if, suddenly, he couldn't get enough of her. He kneaded her flesh, hauling her buttocks apart, his cock nudging into her swollen pussy. He grunted with primitive pleasure when her hungry cunt quickly gave way, sucking him in. He bent over her, sliding in, filling her to the hilt.

"Oh yes." She shuddered with sensation, her hands clawing for the far edge of the table.

"Good?" he murmured against her back. When she moaned agreement, he thrust again, crushing her cervix, circling his hips as if he was testing her for ripeness. "You're so swollen, so sensitive, your cunt is like a hot fist on my cock."

He wasn't kidding. She was already close to coming.

He thrust hard. "Wasn't that worth waiting for?"

She nodded again, awash with sensation, her thighs spreading, her belly flat to the table.

"Ready to be well and truly fucked?"

She opened her mouth to retort, to say she thought she was being fucked already, then she noticed the extent of the tension at her back, like a loaded gun. He hasn't even started, she realized. She bit her lip, braced her arms, and nodded, her head hanging down.

With the precision of a well-oiled machine, he started to move, grinding into her, holding her hips as he drove his cock in and out. She pressed back, meeting each thrust with a low cry, pleasure spilling from her core. He filled her completely. She felt wild, yet tethered. She came fast and hot, her cunt in spasm.

"Nice one, feels good, Lois," he panted. "Ready for more?" He stroked her hair, but he didn't break his stride.

She was his, a rag doll to his will, her body riding the table as he fucked her. Her inner thighs were slick with juices. Her feet were off the floor, heels in the air. Her tits and clit were crushed onto the table, fast growing painful with the push and shove on the hard surface.

And then he thrust harder, swearing when he felt the hot clutch of her body on his. His fists grabbed at her buttocks, manhandling her back against his hips, anchoring her on his cock. He was so deep. Wedged against her cervix, she felt his cock grow larger still. It lurched, spurting. She wriggled and flexed, on the verge of coming again. He squeezed her buttocks, as if milking himself off with her body. Acute sensation roared through her, spiraling out until every part of her was vibrating. She gave a long low moan, her body convulsing.

Against her back, Jack breathed hard. She put her hand over his where it rested on her hip, gratitude welling inside her. She'd never had it this hot before, she'd never taken the time.

He reached for her and kissed her cheek, lifting her and sliding her to her feet, supporting her in his arms. "I'm not done with you yet, Lois. I want to see you perform some more."

She gave a breathy laugh, leaning back against him. "Is that a threat or a promise?"

"Consider it a bit of both."

At the end of her presentation, Lois turned to the gathering and smiled, ready to take questions. Most of the board nodded in agreement. Tim Laybourne rapped his pen on the table, swiveling his gangly head from side to side as he raised the pen in the air to make a point.

Here we go, let's see if Jack's right. She leaned forward and put both hands on the table, flashing her cleavage at him. "Tim, you had a question?" She glanced past him, at Jack, who winked.

Tim coughed uncomfortably, flushing from the top of his collar to the roots of his hair. "I remain unconvinced about the financing of this project." He didn't even sound convinced of his own words. Jack was right; he had the hots, severely.

She eased onto the table, facing in his direction and resting on one hip, her short skirt growing even shorter. She lifted the finance sheet. "The figures don't make sense?" She gave him a gently enquiring smile.

Laybourne stared at her thigh, open-mouthed and speechless.

"If I might interject?" It was Jack, and his expression indicated his restrained humor. "Why don't you just run through that last part again, I'd certainly appreciate a repeat performance." He lifted one eyebrow suggestively.

The tone of his voice and the way he looked at her assured her he wasn't just talking about a run through on the sums. He reached for her again, invisibly nurturing her strengths. She'd always thrived on her role in the workplace, but under his knowing gaze she reveled in it. Since their encounter the week before, everything he'd said to her at work had been laden with suggestion of the sexual kind, keeping their affair on rapid simmer. And right now the tug of his call pulled on her, from cunt to mouth. She was salivating for more of what he'd given her.

"Of course not, Jack. I'm quite sure it would benefit everybody involved."

Jack nodded, his eyes gleaming with affirmation. Then he sat back in his chair and watched her perform, just like he would watch her perform again that night, with measured willpower and the perfect level of restraint, leading to the ultimate mutual reward.

SIGN YOUR NAME

Kind of weird, that's how Molly thought of herself. She told guys that, but mostly they thought she was referring to her attitude or her dress sense, both of which were also kind of weird. She was skittish and wayward, punky, yet quiet and thoughtful. And, it wasn't just that. The thing that got Molly off sexually was pretty unusual too, and she felt it was only fair to let potential lovers know what she needed, upfront. The only way to do that was to show them how it worked. Mostly, they didn't take her seriously. That is, not until Doug came along.

Doug had a spark of curiosity in his bright blue eyes, and a warm, subtle sense of humor. He was intuitive. She liked the way he looked, had done since the day he first walked in to her workplace. He had cropped and spiked black hair, and smiled slow and long, kind of like Mickey Rourke. He ran the secondhand music exchange down the street, and he chose quiet times to come and collect his dry cleaning from the outlet where she worked, times when he remembered that she'd be working her shift -and was just about to shut up shop. He brought her black Nubuck leather jeans, and a multitude of cool Dragonfly shirts, shirts he wouldn't trust to his beat-up old washing machine-or so he said. She'd already warmed to him when he began to chat her up more purposefully.

"You know, Molly," he said, leaning over the countertop to close the gap between them, "we get on so well. Maybe we could go for a drink sometime." He smiled that drawn-out smile, and it made something inside her tick, hopefully.

She put her pen down on the countertop between them, making a line in the space there, and nodded. "Okay."

"Great. Give me your number and we can work out a time." He picked up the pen and flipped over his till receipt, ready to write on the back of it.

Molly stared at the pen in his hand, immediately aroused and self-aware. The key to her kink was right there in his hand. She liked to be written on-in fact it aroused her to the point where she could come from that act alone. This was the time to show him, then she could see how he would react.

She took a deep breath. "Tell you what..." Her voice sounded shaky, and she hated that. She didn't want this to go wrong. She wanted him. Badly. "Why don't you give me your number? It'll be better that way. Really, I promise."

Before he could question her, or show doubt about why she'd said that, she shoved her forearm out across the counter between them, pulling up the sleeve of her top. She ran her finger up and down the soft, sensitive skin on the inside of her forearm. "Write it...here. Please."

Would he laugh at her? One corner of his mouth was still lifted and stayed that way. He toyed with the pen, his eyes assessing. Her breath was trapped in her throat. A moment later he slowly moved one hand and held her wrist down on the counter with it, while he began to write on the spot she had indicated with the other.

His hand around her wrist was warm and strong, sure. And then-oh. The pressure he applied through the ballpoint on her skin made her nerves leap, the sensation chasing itself up her arm and through her body, flooding her with arousal. She bit her lip.

He looked up from the place where he was writing and back at her. She could tell he'd sensed this wasn't just about exchanging numbers. A needy moan escaped her lips.

He stared; one eyebrow lifted, the pen, also. "Did I hurt you?"

"No." She could barely get that one small word out, and when she did, it was with a breathless, relieved sigh. "I like it." She shrugged. "It makes me really hot. I'm wired weird. I just wanted you to know. Up front."

She snatched her arm away, bracing herself for the disbelieving laughter, the snide remark. Tension hung in the air between them, seemingly endless. Then he looked down at the countertop. What was he thinking?

He glanced up. "Kinky girl, huh?"

She stared him directly in the eye, her heart beating fast as she braced herself for rejection. "Does it bother you?"

"Quite the opposite," he replied, and flashed her a grin. "If I know what turns you on, it gives me power... and it just so happens I like to be in charge."

Oh, that made her hot. It was so far from what she had expected him to say, so direct. And then he moved. In a heartbeat, he levered himself over the counter, jumping lithely down onto her side of it. For the first time, he had breached the physical divide between them-and he'd brought the pen with him. Holding it raised in his hand, he put his free hand on her shoulder and walked her through the rails of plastic-covered clothes, backing her toward the wall behind those rails, out of sight of the shop front. He cornered her up against the wall.

Her body pulsed with the thrill of his actions.

He grasped her two hands easily in one of his, and lifted her chin with the pen under her jaw, an action that shot sensation down her neck and chest, right into her hardening nipples. She gasped for breath, her eyes closing and her head moving back to lean against the wall.

"Oh yes, it really does it for you, doesn't it. How bad is it?"

He still had the pen under her jaw, controlling the position of her head and where she could look. Could she tell him? Her eyes were shut and she kept them that way. "I need it." Her voice was a mere murmur. "It's crazy, but I can't come any other way, not the way I do if..."

When her voice trailed off, he moved the pen just enough to apply pressure to the sensitive flesh beneath her jaw. Her eyes flashed open.

"Is this making you wet?"

"Yes."

He was close, staring at her, his eyes bright and focused. The curiosity she had sensed in him had multiplied. He was aroused by her responses; his body shifting close against hers, one knee pressed against the wall at the side of her body.

He gave a soft chuckle. "You know, Molly, I used to wonder about you when I came in here. I liked the way you looked, very pretty but different, and always thinking...always with the sexy eyes. There was something else though, wasn't there. You were always playing with your pen, always sucking on the end of it. Couldn't just be ready for the next customer, I figured. Couldn't quite work out what it was, but it made me hard just watching you play with the damn thing." His voice turned husky, right at the end there.

"Are you hard now?" She flashed her eyes, her responses rolling out readily.

His grip on her wrists tightened and he moved the back of her contained hands against the zipper on his jeans. "Well, what do you think?"

Beneath the black denim he wore, his cock was rigid.

Her skin tingled with awareness when he brushed it over that spot. She nodded. He moved the pen, lifting it

28

from beneath her jaw and taking it down to the hem of her miniskirt. Putting it under the fabric and between her thighs, he tapped it from side to side then up and down, making her thighs tremble with the need for a deeper mark, the pressure, and the stain-the written evidence on her body.

He let go her wrists, and lifted her skirt right up, exposing her. "Ooh, white cotton panties. Just like a blank page."

She stepped from one foot in the other, wired. "You're torturing me," she breathed.

"Maybe this will help." He ran the pen down the front of her panties, pushing both pen and fabric into the groove of her pussy.

Her flesh blazed under that touch. She glanced down to look at the solid line he had drawn, but he was still moving the pen, pressing deeper into her groove, rolling over her clit. When she gave a sudden gasp, he paused and concentrated on the same spot, drawing back and forth over it. A jaggedy blue scribble was forming right over the spot.

"You like that?"

Her clit was swollen and pounding, the direct stimulation hitting her hard. She nodded. "Very much."

He did it some more.

Her hands and head were flat to the wall, her hips jutting out towards him. "Oh yes, yes," she said, pounding the palm of one hand against the wall as she came, her free hand reaching out for his shoulder to steady herself.

She was about to speak, to say something, when she heard the door opening in the shop front, and hurriedly pulled her skirt straight. He stepped to one side, pointing down with the pen he held, possessively. "I want those panties, you better keep them for me."

"Maybe." She smiled. She wanted them too. "You only gave me half of your number," she added, concerned that he might leave now.

He spanked her on the behind playfully, smiling that smile of his. "Fuck that. You're coming home with me tonight."

A month later, Molly's foible had been well and truly exploited. Before Doug, she'd fretted about her route to sexual pressure. Doug had all but mended that in her, and now he was adding his own spin. He was fascinated with her odd little needs, and he'd written on just about every part of her body, watching her, enjoying her-wanking with one hand or fucking her hard while he gave her exactly what she wanted. Afterwards, he tended her carefully, bathing her and massaging away the telltale signs of her kink.

That made her feel cherished, safe.

He asked her to move in with him. She said she'd think about it. He didn't press her on the subject. Instead, he continued to show her that those kind-of-weird needs of hers would never be forgotten. He took her back to his place and told her he was going to kick it up a notch. The way he said it scared her and thrilled her at the same time.

Shortly after, she found herself naked and blindfolded, standing with her back against the wall, her hands splayed either side of her-just as he had instructed. Keyed up to the max, she shifted anxiously, unable to stay still. She'd never been blindfolded before, but the velvet covering her eyes was soft as a sigh, a shield that raised the awareness of her every other sense. Her body ached for contact, for pleasure and relief.

She could sense him moving.

The room was virtually silent and the air was still, but she knew he was treading softly, watching her and making a plan. That was his way. Maybe she'd sensed that in him when she'd watched him across the counter. It was his curiosity, and his intensity, that had spiked her interest. Rightly so, as it turned out.

She heard a click and a fan whirred into action. A moment later the air brushed over her alert skin, tantalizingly. A whimper escaped her.

He began to hum under his breath, then he sang to her huskily. It was a song she loved. Breathless, aroused laughter escaped her; she felt delirious under his spell. "Dougie, please, you're playing with me."

"Always, sweetheart, but you love that."

He was so right. She squeezed her thighs together, scared to say more, and scared to ruin this.

"Will it drive you mad, not being able to see where I choose to write on you?"

"I don't know." She swallowed. "Maybe." She turned her face away, desperate with longing for that first touch, the pressure she craved-her skin was crawling with the need for it. Watching him write on her was half the pleasure, she thought. Not seeing it was an unknown quantity. But Doug knew and understood that, and-now-so did she.

Slowly, he drew a line around each wrist.

Her arms trembled with the sheer intensity of sensation that shot along the surface of her skin, and deeper.

"Shackles." His voice was a murmur close to her. "Because I want you to be mine." He kissed her throat and then, slowly, with great deliberation, he signed his name right across her breastbone.

"Oh. Oh, oh," she cried. The intense sensation shot beneath her skin, wiring her whole body into the experience. Her nipples were hard and hurting. She shuddered with arousal, her toes curling, her heart thudding against the wall of her chest.

His next move came out of nowhere. He drew along the crease at the top of one thigh, then the other. The sudden deep stimulation in a place so sensitive, primed her for release. She longed to see his marks on her.

"The inside of your thighs are wet, right down to here." There was admiration in his voice. Restraint, too. He touched her with the pen, briefly, between her thighs, and it made her squirm up against the wall.

"Face the wall," he instructed, his voice husky.

She turned.

His cock brushed against her buttock. "There's a box to your left, step onto it."

She moved her foot, felt her way. He guided her up onto the box.

"Offer yourself to me."

Understanding hit her; he was going to fuck her there up against the wall, while she stood there on a box, blindfolded. This was Doug; this is how he liked to have her, to be in charge of her. Hands braced against the wall, she spread her feet, pushing her bottom up and out, angling herself against the wall.

"Oh yes, I like you this way, on a pedestal, all ready for me." His cock moved between her thighs.

The box put her right at the height he needed to glide up into her. Anticipation had her in its grip. She was breathing so fast she felt dizzy. Picturing the shackles he had drawn on her wrists, she splayed her fingers on the wall, knowing she'd need to anchor herself-he got kind of wild when he was inside her. He was humming again now, and she wondered what he'd done with the pen. Was it in his mouth while he arranged her to his satisfaction?

He stroked her pussy, opening her up. His fingers moved with ease, slick, sliding in against her wetness. With two digits, he opened her up to his cock. The intensity of being felt, held, and displayed that way on a pedestal all at once took her breath away. With one hand around her

32

hips, he thrust the thick shaft of his erection inside her. It filled her completely, taking her breath away. Her legs wavered.

Where is his other hand? The thought echoed around her mind frantically.

Then she found out.

Even as he thrust into her, in shallow quick maneuvers, keeping her in place, he began to write down her spine with his free hand.

It was almost too much. Her shoulders wriggled and her pussy clamped on his shaft. Her stomach flipped and sweat broke out on her skin. She would have staggered, if he hadn't got her pinned by his cock. She panted out loud, her mouth opening, her body clenching on him rhythmically.

"Oh yes, that's good," he said, keeping the pen moving in around her spine, working his way down her back. "This makes you so wild, you're going to squeeze my cock until I come."

"Can't control it," she whispered, head hanging down.

"That's the way I like it," he grunted.

By the time the pen reached her tailbone, she was a panting wreck on the verge of climax. He drew a wobbly heart there at the base of her spine, following the shape around and around with his pen. The action and her response were mesmerizing, and when her climax hit it lasted long, easing off only to return in a rush when he grew rigid and jerked, coming deep inside her.

They stayed that way until his cock finally slid free, and then he untied the blindfold and lifted her into his arms, carrying her toward the bathroom.

She squinted up at him, clinging to him. Kissing his shoulder, his throat and when he turned towards her, his mouth, she felt grateful to have found her perfect opposite. She was still trembling from the intensity of her release.

"This is one of my favorite parts, scrubbing you down afterwards, my dirty girl."

"It gets you going again," she teased, smiling at him.

"You're not wrong there."

Inside the bathroom, he stood her on the bath mat, and reached for the taps. While the bath filled, he traced his finger across her chest, following the line of his name that he had written there earlier. "So, you'll move in with me?"

She shivered, an echo of her orgasm tingling from the core of her body to the tip of her spine. "Yes."

"Good," he replied, nonchalantly. "Ever thought about having a tattoo?"

She saw the humor in his eyes. He hadn't made a big deal of her moving in, just as he hadn't made a big deal about her kink that first day. He'd come to understand her, very quickly. "Having a tattoo would probably kill me, and you know it," she replied.

"Hell of a way to go, though," he mused, as he lifted her into the bath.

The warm water moved in and around her legs and hips, melting her. After he scrubbed her down, he would climb in with her. That was one of her favorite parts.

He kneeled down beside the bath and reached for the sponge. "If you ever do have a tattoo, I want to be the one who is inside you while you're having it done. Is that a deal?"

She reached her hand around his head, drawing him in for a kiss. "It's a deal," she whispered.

RICHARD'S SECRET

"A gimp?" Richard was a sex slave? Could it be possible? I swallowed, breathed deep and tried to make sense of what Tom had just told me. "But what does it mean??" I looked up at him, spluttering the words out. "I mean, I know what it means... I just don't know what he means by it, by approaching us."

Tom rested his hand reassuringly on my shoulder. There was a look of deep concern in his eyes and he was watching me carefully for my reactions. Oh, how I loved this man; when he had said he had something "a bit heavy" to talk to me about, I thought the worst was about to happen, that he was going to say there was another woman, that he was leaving me. The last thing I expected was for him to reveal this, Richard's secret. Richard's darkest secret.

I had actually known Richard longer than I had my lover, Tom. Richard had been working in the international trade department when I was transferred to the London branch, about six years earlier. Admittedly Richard was the dark horse in the department, and the office gossips plagued him with questions about his private life, all of which he managed to avoid and dismiss without being in the least bit offensive.

To me Richard was just a shy, reclusive guy; a small man, and very attractive in an understated way-nicely packaged, dark hair and vivid blue eyes. I just assumed he was comfortable around me because I was the only one who didn't quiz him about his private life. That was also how I had learned more about him than the tenacious office gossips. He lived alone in an apartment overlooking the Thames and enjoyed a number of extreme sports;

acute and prolonged bouts of mountain biking, martial arts and kick boxing. I supposed that's what gave him his good packaging-the guy worked out, you know-but none of that seemed to go with his shy, understated image. Neither did this fetishistic sexuality that I had just learned about, but then... maybe it did kind of make sense?

I had kept the personal information he gave me to myself, which is why he liked me, I assumed; he appreciated that kind of mutual respect. Now that I reflected on it, I guess he had been even friendlier to me since Tom had arrived on the work scene, and when he and I had moved in together, two years ago; but shy single men often feel more comfortable around women who are attached. Little did I know he was observing Tom and me with this kind of proposal in mind. He wanted to be our sex slave, our gimp. My heart rate had gone up several notches and my body was hot, almost uncomfortably hot. I fanned myself with a magazine while trying to come to terms with the conundrum, and the rather extreme affect it was having on me-I had to admit it, the idea made me horny as hell.

"Suzie, I can see you are interested, my love." Tom folded his arms. He was standing in front of me and nodded down at my breasts, where my nipples were swollen and crushed beneath the surface of my silk blouse. There was no hiding it. My sex was clenching, my body was on fire.

"Yes, I can't deny it... the idea of it makes me hot, but you know...I want us to be ok." I eyed up his long, lean body, the fall of his dark blonde hair on his neck. I couldn't bear to lose this man... hell; I could hardly get through a day without wanting to meld our bodies together and fuck each other senseless.

"It won't affect anything between us, it's just an adventure." He began to stroke my face, pushing back my hair where it was sticking to the damp heat of my neck.

"He said he will be transferring soon, so there wouldn't be any awkwardness afterwards, at work, it would just be a one-off." My, he had thought of everything, and he'd obviously been planning the whole thing for quite a while, too. Tom lifted my chin with one finger, his thumb stroking gently over my lower lip. "He said it would be up to us, he said we could do what we wanted with him." There was a dark, suggestive look in Tom's eyes.

"I see..." I mumbled, not sure if I did.

"One thing I'd like to see..." His voice was hoarse. He ran a finger down the collar of my blouse and into my cleavage. He slipped one finger inside, pulling the blouse open, looking at the shadow between my breasts. His other hand lifted mine and led it to his groin, where his cock was already hard inside his jeans.

"What?" I wanted to know. The blood was rushing in my ears; the magazine in my hand fell to the floor.

"I'd like to watch him going down on you." His eyes were filled with lust. I groaned, my hips beginning to shift as I rocked back and forth on the hard kitchen stool I was sitting on, my sex hungry for action. He leaned forward and kissed me, his tongue plunging into my mouth. My fingers fumbled with his fly buttons, and then I was bringing his heavy cock out and stroking it with my whole hand. He pushed me backwards, over the breakfast bar. He was going to fuck me, right there and then, and I was ready; Sweet Jesus was I ready. I hoisted my skirt up around my hips. He dragged my knickers off and pushed my thighs apart with rough, demanding movements. He stroked my inflamed clit, growling when he saw the juices dribbling from my blushing slit. Then he fucked me while I perched on the kitchen stool, pivoting on its hard surface with everything on display.

"Get your tits out," he whispered, as he thrust his cock deep inside me, his body crouched over me. I pulled my blouse open, my hands shaking as they shoved my breasts together, kneading them and tweaking the nipples, sending vibrant shivers through my core. I was whimpering, jammed down on his thrusting cock as hard as I could in my position. Tom watched with hungry eyes as I crushed my breasts. I suddenly remembered Richard blushing when I had caught him looking at me over his monitor, just the other day. Was he aroused then? Had his cock got hard when he'd been thinking about me and Tom? He had glanced away, furtively, his color high. Dear god, the man had been thinking about us doing this; maybe even thinking about doing this with us. He had told Tom his dark secret, and Tom was now rutting me like a wild man. I was on fire. I whimpered, my hands suddenly clutching at Tom's shoulders. I was about to come, I had never come so bloody fast in my entire life.

"You look very beautiful, Suzie," Richard said. My fingers fidgeted with my neckline, nervously. "I always thought you looked like Audrey Hepburn with your hair up like that." He smiled; he seemed quite calm now, and he was leading the situation even though he was going to be the slave. We were nervous, but then we were the novices, presumably he had done this many times before. I glanced at Tom. He had chatted happily about work while we made our way through several glasses of wine, until now-until Richard had moved the conversation on to a personal note. Now Tom had grown silent and watchful.

"Thank you," I replied, swigging another mouthful of wine. Both men were staring at me; the sexual tension had risen dramatically. "It's the little black dress," I added, with a smile. That morning I had told myself that I wasn't dressed any differently; I always wore stockings, garters and high heels to the office. The little black dress underneath my jacket was the new addition. It was very soft and clingy, and now that I had abandoned the jacket I felt good in it. Besides, what does one wear when one is about to take on a sex slave?

"You want to know what I've got in the briefcase, don't you?" Richard had seen me looking at his black leather briefcase when we had left the office that evening, the three of us going back to our place for drinks. Yes, I had been curious. I nodded. "I like to wear a mask," he said. "I've brought it with me and I'd like you to put it on for me."

The combination of power and deviance he had suggested in that simple comment hit my libido like a heady narcotic entering the bloodstream. The pulse in my sex pounded.

"Ok, I'll do it," I replied, as nonchalantly as I could manage.

Richard stood up, taking off his immaculate suit jacket as he did so, and placing it over the arm of the sofa. He picked up the black leather briefcase and carried it over to the breakfast bar, where he set it down, flicked the combination lock and opened it. Tom and I both watched with bated breath. Richard undid his tie, rolling it slowly and tucking into a section in the top of the briefcase. Then he lifted something out of the case and turned back towards us, leaving the briefcase sitting, open, on the breakfast bar. As he walked back to me I stood up.

"It's perfectly safe," he said, allaying any concerns we might have in advance. "It was hand made, for me." He passed the soft, black leather mask into my hand. I turned it, feeling it with my fingers. It was cool to the touch and incredibly soft, molded, with laces down the back and breathing holes for the nose, a closed zip over the mouth. A powerful jolt went through me when I realized that there were no eye holes; Richard would not be able to see what we were doing once he had the mask on. My eyes flitted quickly to Tom and I saw that he had noticed that too. Richard undid his shirt revealing well muscled shoulders and torso. He dropped it on the sofa and stood in his black pants, looking from one to the other of us, for our consent.

"Turn around, and I'll put it on." Even as I heard my own voice another wave of empowerment roared over me. Richard smiled slightly and inclined his head.

Tom suddenly stood up. "I think you should take that dress off, first," he instructed. The mask dangled from my hand. Richard's eyelids fell as he looked at the floor, hanging his head, but I could see that he was smiling to himself. The atmosphere positively hummed with sexual tension. Tom's instruction had completed the dynamics of the triangle. This was it; the scene was set for action.

I put the mask down on the coffee table and pulled the soft jersey dress up and over my head.

"You can take one look at her, before she puts your mask on." Tom's eyes glittered. Richard's head moved as he looked back over to my stiletto-heeled shoes, up to my stockings and the scrap of fine French lace barely covering my crotch, then up and on to the matching balconette bra that confined my breasts. I knew I looked statuesque and glamorous in this, my most expensive underwear, and I could see that he approved.

"Thank you," he said, his eyes sinking to the floor again. Before he turned his back he passed something else into Tom's hands. It was a set of intricately carved manacles. As Tom looked down at the object, Richard turned his back, bent his head and put his wrists behind his back-awaiting both the mask and the manacles. Not only would he not be able to see, he wouldn't be able to touch. Tom looked at me, his eyebrows lifting, a wicked smile teasing the corners of his mouth.

Tom stepped over and enclosed Richard's strong wrists in the manacles. Then it was my turn to take action and I closed on him, heart pounding, and began to ease the mask over his head. It pulled easily into place and I gently tightened the laces, gauging my way until the mask was molded, tight and secure over his face. When the knot was done Richard slowly descended to the floor, squatting down on his knees; eyes unseeing, his head cocked, as if awaiting instructions.

We circled him, taking in the look of this creature, as he had now become, kneeling between us in the centre of our personal space. I had prepared the room well, with the furniture pushed back and subdued lighting. He knelt between us with his masked head lifted up and back, his strong arms manacled behind him, his cock a discernible hard outline in his pants. With Tom towering over him, Richard presented an image I would never forget.

Tom nodded at me, pushed an armchair forward and indicated that I sit down.

"Do you remember what I said?" He kissed me, then pulled my knickers down the length of my legs and up, over my heels, stroking my ankles as he did so. I nodded. "Good." He smiled-it was devastating, wicked-and then he grabbed our slave around the back of the neck and urged him forward. "Your mistress is one horny bitch. I want you to go down on her, and make sure you do the job properly. I'll be watching." With that, he unzipped the mouth on the mask and slowly lowered Richard's head into the heat between my thighs.

I couldn't believe this was happening-Tom was so dominant, so strong and commanding. I was getting wetter by the second. I couldn't look down at the man between my thighs; I felt a sudden rush of embarrassment and strangeness as he crouched there, unseeing and yet so sexual. My gaze followed Tom as he moved away. He was looking into the briefcase that had been left open on the breakfast bar. What was in the briefcase, I wondered, again. Then I felt the surface of the mask, cold against my

41

thighs as Richard moved his head along them, feeling his way toward the hot niche at their juncture. The tip of his tongue stuck out and I felt its blissful touch in the sticky, cloying heat of my slit. He used his tongue like a digit, exploring the territory of my sex, before he began mouthing me, his tongue lapping against my swollen lips and over the jutting flesh of my clit. It felt so good; my embarrassment was quickly replaced by something else: sheer rampant lust. I tried to stay calm and take my time; I had to resist the urge to gyrate on the edge of the seat and push myself into his obedient face.

After a moment I became aware of Tom's presence again and looked up, gasping for breath. He had stripped off his shirt, his leanly muscled chest bared for my eager eyes. I purred; he blew me a kiss, and then grinned.

"Stop now." At the sound of the order Richard's head lifted, cocking to one side again. "I've found some of your other toys and I intend to use them. Do you understand?" Richard nodded. My fingers clutched over my clit, replacing the tongue, keeping me on the edge while I tried to see the objects Tom was holding in his hands.

He pocketed a shiny blue condom packet, and gestured at Richard with a stiff leather object. Tom looked dangerous now. He always had a certain edginess about him during sex, but I'd never seen him quite this intense before.

"You really are a deviant one, aren't you?" He gave a deep chuckle. Richard hung his head in shame. "Oh, but there's no need to be so embarrassed, we can both see you've got a stiffy, Richard." With that he crouched down on the floor and grabbed at Richard's belt. He opened the buckle, the button and zipper in the blink of an eye and, yes, he did have a stiffy-a major stiffy.

"You are a bad boy, and did you get hard when you had a taste of Suzie?" He nodded. "Right, I'm going to have to take care of this, no one said you were allowed to get a hard-on did they?" He pulled Richard so he was kneeling straight up, his pants falling down around his knees. He wasn't wearing underwear and my eyes roved over him in appreciation. Tom pushed his head to one side and bent down, his hand measuring the other man's cock in a hard vigorous fist. God, what a sight! I shot two fingers inside my slit, probing myself while I watched Tom handle Richard's cock.

With some effort, he pushed the cock harness over Richard's erection and secured it with the stud fastener around his balls. He was almost entirely covered. I could just see his balls squeezed up inside the circles of leather, and the very head of his cock pushing out of its containment. The harness was extremely tight and I could see the effect it was having on Richard, his whole body growing more rigid by the second, as if he was being gripped in a hard heavy hand, his blood-filled cock bursting for release.

"Get back to work on Suzie, right now." Tom pushed him back between my thighs. By then I was on the very edge of the chair, my legs spread wide to get more of him. Tom walked behind him and pulled the condom out of his pocket, turning it over in his hands. He looked at me; his green eyes glittered like gemstones. His eyebrows lifted imperceptibly and his mouth was fixed in a devilish smile. He wanted my approval. I whimpered, my head barely nodding, but I really wanted to see him doing it. Tom opened his flies and got out his rock hard cock. He pumped it in his hands for a moment, his eyes on mine. It was one of my favorite sights; I couldn't get enough of seeing him with his hands on his cock, and he knew it. He looked down at my chest, growling. I followed his gaze and saw that my nut hard nipples were jutting up from the edges of my bra, my breasts oozing out of the restraining fabric.

Tom eased the condom on and then knelt down behind Richard. When Richard felt his legs being pushed apart his mouth stopped moving and clamped over my sex. His body was rigid between us, his buttocks on display to Tom, his face pushing in against my sex, his muscled arms bound tightly behind his back. If I rolled my head to one side I could see his harnessed cock.

He remained quite still, his tongue in my hole when Tom began to probe him from behind. Tom's face contorted and I felt Richard's head thrust in against me as he was entered from behind. My hips were moving fast on the chair, moving my desperate sex flesh up and down against the leather mask, his mouth and the rough edges of the zipper. I couldn't help it, I was gone on this.

Richard's cock looked fit to burst. Tom pulled out and ploughed deeper, his teeth bared with effort and restraint. He must have hit the spot, because Richard's body tensed and arched, his tongue going soft and limp against my clit. I glanced down and saw his cock riding high and tight in its harness, then it spurted up under his arched body, which was convulsing.

"You made him come," I cried accusingly, but with delight, and a dark laugh choked in my throat. Tom grinned at me and then jammed into him hard again.

"Suck her good, Richard; I want Suzie to come next."

Our obedient slave began to tongue me again. I gasped my pleasure aloud for Tom-Tom, my gorgeous lover, he was watching me. It was just like our sessions of mutual masturbation, but with Richard's darkest secret filling the void between us; tonight he was the gap across which we watched each other's deepest pleasures rising up and taking us over.

Tom's lean body was taut, his hands gripping onto Richard's hips, the sinuous muscles in his arms turning to rope. His eyes were locked on mine, urging me on as he sent Richard latching over my clit again with each deep thrust. I began to buck, wildly out of control, shock waves going right through the core of my body and under the skin of my scalp as wave after wave of relief flooded over me, and then Tom threw back his head, roaring his release as his hips jerked repeatedly.

Tom sat across the breakfast bar from me. He sipped the rich black Colombian coffee I had made us, his fingertips running against mine as he eyed me over his cup. He smiled as he put the cup down and lifted my fingers to his lips.

"You looked incredible," he whispered, kissing my fingertips. It was an extremely intimate moment; he was looking at me with possessiveness and something akin to awe.

"So did you," I replied and I meant it; I was overwhelmed by my lover. Richard had long since left us, but the images he had given us of each other would be with us for a very long time.

"Do you think we'll ever see him again?"

"Maybe," he replied. "Maybe not. Would it bother you if we did?"

I gave it some thought. I pictured us casually speaking to him in the office, the way we used to, but this time the three of us would be looking at each other and knowing what had gone on. The idea of it made my pulse quicken again.

"No, not in the least." I liked the idea. I smiled at Tom. Not only had we seen each other anew, but Tom and I had become part of Richard's secret, part of Richard's darkest secret.

UNLEASHED

SASKIA WALKER

HUNGRY FOR LOVE

I'm so hungry for you.

We flirt across the restaurant table and our food, while I sit there thinking about what we're going to do when we're finally alone. It's a favorite pastime of mine, but you know that, don't you? And you love every minute of it because it gets me so wet. In fact, you'll find out just how wet it's getting me when you touch me there, later.

You watch me eat-your direct, observant stare sending a shiver of anticipation under my skin. The electricity crackles between us. I idle over mental images of your naked body while I imagine how you'll use it tonight. Your hand moves to your wineglass, I watch and wonder if that hand will cup my naked buttock as you ease me onto your erect cock. I can almost feel your chest, pressed against my naked breasts. I'm very wet now; my panties are cleaving to the groove of my sex. If you could feel that, would you savor it, or ram your cock home? I rearrange myself on the chair, my sex responding, aching with need. The movement catches your attention. You look directly at me, an accusing glint in your eye.

My pulse rate nudges higher. I speculate some more, knowing that you're observing me even more closely. With one finger, I trace the line of my shirt where it dips into my cleavage, your eyes following. Will you suck my tits and explore my sex with your fingers? Will you undress me slowly, observantly, or barely bother to take anything off? What would you do if I said I wanted that?

I've given up eating. How hungry will I be for you by the time we get to each other? How loud will you moan when I go down on your cock?

47

You fold your napkin. You refuse the dessert menu, asking for the bill instead.

I'm thrilled.

You whisper that I look as if butter wouldn't melt in my mouth, but you're willing to bet it'll melt elsewhere.

I like your suggestion for dessert. I smile and stand up.

You grasp me against you as we leave, your hand sliding possessively around my hip.

My heart races as our time alone draws near. Will you beg me to sit on your face while I give you head? Will you lead me to bed, or have me fast and furious up against the wall, my skirt up around my waist, my panties hanging on one ankle. Or better still, will you turn me around and bend me over a chair, giving me your cock hard to quickly relieve this fast-growing tension between us? How will you react when I tell you what it's doing to me? And you know that I will tell you, loud and dirty. I'll ask you to fuck me harder, if I want it that way.

Outside the restaurant, you turn into a dark alleyway and snatch me against you, kissing me hot and hard, your tongue thrusting into my mouth, your hand under my skirt, backing me against the wall.

You groan and murmur admonishments when you feel my wetness, your fingers delving into my black lace panties to explore me.

God, that's good.

Hauling your hand out, you taste me and then tell me to turn around and lean up against the wall. When I do, you nudge my legs further apart with one powerful knee.

I shudder, my legs weak with desire.

You tell me how dirty I am, you tell me that you could see what I was thinking a mile off. You ask me how you were supposed to enjoy your food with this horny slut creaming her seat in front of you.

I shake my head, my body flushed with heat, my hips arching back, inviting you in. I hear your zipper; feel your cock nudging against me.

I'm on fire for it.

You strip my panties down my thighs. You ask me again, you want to hear me say it aloud.

I tell you that I was hungry most of all for love.

You lift my hips, feeding me a length of your cock, asking me yet again, knowing I'm desperate.

I cry out for your cock, begging you to give it to me.

You ram home, filling me to overflowing, quickly surging into me over again.

I come moments later, my body shoved up against the wall with the force of your attack. I cry out in sheer bliss, the sound echoing around the dark alley.

You whisper in my ear that this dessert option will have you coming back again. You say you intend to take a portion home.

I smile, clutch you against me and tell you I'm glad, because my hunger for this only seems to grow.

UNLEASHED

THE LUNCH BREAK

"What can I get you?"

I glanced up from my pocket mirror and when I saw the attractive waitress who watched and waited, I was so startled that I dropped my lipstick. Her gaze was direct, fearless and powerfully sexual. My body responded instantly, my pulse rate rising.

"Coffee, please, and a club sandwich." I scrabbled for the lipstick. Her eyes never left mine, but she leaned down to the table and shifted the ashtray, nudging the lipstick back in my direction.

"Oh, I just bet you take your coffee sweet and strong," she whispered, low.

"Yes," I replied, mesmerized. "I do."

She gave me a dazzling smile then turned and walked away, her hips cutting a rhythmic path through the low-slung tables and chairs in the sedate lounge bar. I sat back and watched, my fingers toying idly with the fitted jacket of my business suit, which lay abandoned over the arm of the chair. I had stopped in at Kilpatrick's, the salubrious and rather austere London hotel, after the meeting with my client, the hotel's publicity officer. He was sold on my advertising proposals and I was on a high. I just knew that if I had gotten behind the wheel of my Land Rover in that state, I'd have picked up another speeding ticket, so I stayed on to chill for a while. With the attention I was now getting from the waitress, it looked as if chilling wasn't going to be an option.

When she delivered my order she threw me another look filled with pure, raw, sex appeal. She turned my cup in its saucer, facing the handle towards me. Her name badge announced that she was called Martine.

"I'm testing out some new cocktails for the bar, why don't you drop by before you leave and I'll give you a taste of something good." She winked. *Well, that was direct.* I felt the tug of the woman's invitation from the pit of my stomach to the tip of my clit.

"Thanks, I'll do that, Martine."

I mustered a nonchalant smile, my fingers ruffling through my short, cherry-dyed crop, and watched as she walked away, her hips skirting obstacles. She knew that I watched. She stretched her legs back as she bent over the tables, the scalloped edge of her black skirt brushing tantalizingly, high against the back of her thighs, offering a glimpse of what appeared to be stocking tops. Her body was lush and curvy, her mouth a ruby pout. She cast sidelong glances back to me, her finger flicking quickly against the corners of her bow tie, before smoothing slowly over her fitted waistcoat.

I barely touched the sandwich; my appetite had been redirected toward the waitress. I had never been approached by a woman as forthright and blatant as her before -or as glamorous. It was one of those rare encounters when fizzing chemistry instantly anchors two people together. The situation made me very hot, but could I act on it? I was supposed to be in work mode. What the hell. Of course I could act on it!

Martine smiled and her eyes flashed a welcome from under heavy eyelashes when I climbed onto the bar stool in front of her. She was a total sexbomb, with thickly fringed, dark brown eyes and blue-black hair clipped up at the back of her head. The occasional glossy coil escaped to hang tantalizingly over her eyes, giving her subtle cover as she glanced around. There were signs of an alternative edge beneath her smart uniform. She had an electric blue streak in her hair; both her ears were fully studded and there was evidence of a nose piercing. I liked that. I also had a streak of die-hard glam-punk that refused to conform, despite my career. Through the thin white sleeves of her shirt, I could make out her tattoos flexing as she went about her business behind the bar, rapidly shaking a cocktail mixer in such a physical way that her figure was shown off to perfection. I imagined what it would feel like to be pressed hard against her, to rub against her naked breasts and touch her in between those strong thighs. Maybe we would exchange contact details. Maybe we could meet, later on. My sex was heavy with the idea of it, the sensitive flesh crushed inside my G-string plump and swollen.

Martine set up a tall glass in front of me, gave the cocktail mixer a final dramatic shake and poured me out a long, tall drink over crackling ice, popping in a smart black swizzle stick. She rested two provocatively speared cherries on the edge of the glass at the last moment, then pushed it over.

"A new recipe, please have some...and tell me what you think. Compliments of the bar." She gave me another wink. Her accent was heavy, either French or Italian.

I sipped the vibrant red-orange drink, looking at the waitress over the two plump cherries. Martine watched; her lips slightly open, a devilish look in her eyes. The cocktail hit the back of my throat; it was ice cold and zappy, exhilarating. I could taste cranberry juice and other fruits-grenadine, vodka and something else, a mystery ingredient I could not identify.

"Mmmm...what is it?"

"It is Martine's version of Sex On The Beach," she replied, putting one hand on her hip and the other elbow on the bar, resting her chin on her hand as she looked directly into my eyes. "Shall we call it...Sex In My Bedroom?"

She is definitely coming on to me.

I felt a rush of heat traversing my body, right from the tips of my toes to the roots of my hair. Was it the affect of the cocktail, or the provocative woman who had made it for me?

"Do you think you'd like that? sex in my bedroom?" she added, her voice low.

Wow, direct wasn't the word. My heart was racing. I breathed deep, trying to order my thoughts. I had never had such a direct come-on-this was one express lady. What would she be like in bed?

"I think I'd like to try it," I replied.

Martine's mouth slid into another wide grin. "I'm due my lunch break."

I almost dropped the glass on the bar. She meant now? I glanced at my watch. I was due back at the office in just over an hour. I had promised to catch Jack, my boss, before he left for a board meeting. Martine toyed with a swizzle stick, eyeing my cleavage. My body thundered out its response.

"Okay," I managed. "Let's do it."

She turned to the barman working the other end of the bar and called out some instructions to him in French. He nodded and waved. She turned back to me, her eyes smoldering. God, she was hot. I wanted to find out exactly how hot.

"Come to room fourteen, lower ground floor, in three minutes." She pulled up a key chain from her hip, put a key into the register and logged herself off. "I have only forty minutes for lunch break though," she added, lifting her eyebrows suggestively.

Perfect. I could be back at work in time.

The three minutes seemed to drag, but gave me enough time to consider taking flight. I stayed put. Just a few minutes earlier, I had been reflecting on my business meeting. Now, well, now I was on Martine's lunch break with her. I glanced at my watch and swore low under my breath. It was time. I threw back the rest of the drink and stood up.

I clutched my jacket and portfolio against my chest and hurried down the stairs marked "Staff Only." I couldn't quite believe I was doing it, lurking in the hidden corridors of a premier London hotel, heading to an illicit meeting with a sexbomb with whom I had exchanged only a handful of words. A deviant thrill fired my veins.

Perhaps I would wake up.

And then there it was, room 14. From inside I could hear the distinct and powerful drum and bass sound of industrial dance music. I took a deep breath.

"Come on in," a voice shouted out, when I rapped on the door. I turned the handle and pushed the door open. The room was filled with clutter, a metal-framed bed surrounded with stacks of clothes and teetering piles of books; lamps, bric-a-brac and cushions covered the spaces between. Even the walls were covered with posters, photographs, mirrors and other paraphernalia. A scarlet sarong was draped across the metal head of the bed, a vivid dash of color in the gloom. Over the bed, a poster of Annie Lennox at her most androgynous grinned cheekily down from the wall. In the center of it all was Martine, sitting on the bed with her legs coiled under her. She chuckled, leapt up and walked over. She rested one hand on my bare upper arm, stroking me, sending wild threads of electricity between us. I caught a breath of her perfume, something musky.

"What do they call you, Red?" She nodded up to my hair.

"Kim," I replied, smiling.

"Kim, huh? well, Kim, I like a woman who goes after what she wants." Her tone was admiring.

Wait a minute. Me? Did I really go after her?

I had responded to her, I couldn't deny that, and I'd found my way down the stairs, so I guess I was guilty.

Martine growled low in her throat, eyeing my body. The atmosphere positively crackled between us.

"I admire your directness, too," I replied. "Thank you for your invitation, it made me very hot."

Martine grinned, proudly, and pulled me into the room by one arm, closing in on my mouth for an urgent kiss as the door slammed shut. Her mouth was lush and hot, damp and inviting. My portfolio clattered to the floor. She backed me towards the bed, her eyes sparkling.

"You have to do it, when it happens like this, yes, or you will have a regret, and life it is too short for regrets, huh?"

She flickered her eyebrows at me. Before I had a chance to reply, she pushed me back and I landed on the bed on my back. She moved like lightening, her hands homing in on the heat of my sex, to the wetness that she knew awaited her. I opened my legs, my skirt riding up.

"Take your clothes off, quickly!"

I stripped off my skirt and started to pull my top up and over my head while Martine pulled my silk G-string down my legs. The shelves behind us rattled and something fell, the stereo jumped onto the next track. My blood surged with a dangerous, dizzy rush of exhilaration when Martine stroked my legs and moved straight into my heat, taking my clit in her mouth, nursing its fullness and sucking deeply. She moved her mouth over my flesh in deliberate sweeps, ending back on my clitoris, with the tip of her tongue circling it closely, firmly. Oh, she was good. I felt as if a bomb was about to go off inside me.

That's when I noticed the mirror that stood close alongside the bed and the scene reflected there transfixed me-the two of us, in profile. Martine was kneeling between my legs and as her skirt rode up, I saw she wore stockings but no panties, her pussy naughtily peeping out as she bent between my legs. I could just make out the tip of her tongue, darting out and rolling over my sticky sex folds. It looked so strange, seeing myself like that, with her on me, and it sent me flying toward meltdown point.

"Oh fuuuuuck."

Martine lifted her head. Her fingers replaced her mouth and she plowed them inside me. Her free hand crept up to my bra, and she bent its cups down, setting my breasts free.

"You want it don't you?" she asked, as her fingers tweaked at my nipples, bringing me nearer. She kicked off her shoes and slid her body down with her pussy pressed up against my bare thigh.

"Oh fuck," I murmured again, when I felt the beautiful wet slide of Martine's heat on my leg. A wave of pleasure rushed up, the first ebbs of my orgasm.

"You're so hot," she said and her eyes were aflame. She began to move her hips pressing her sex along my thigh, rubbing frantically. "I'm going to come too!"

We exchanged a look of total mutual appreciation, both moving desperately, climbing over the threshold. I let my hands close tightly on Martine's shoulders and pressed my leg up into the hot wet valley of flesh that rode me. Martine's lips parted and her eyes closed. She ground her hips down and pressed home. With a sudden cry, she came. My core pounded with release, my clit a buzz of sensation.

After a few moments of labored breathing, my head rolled to look back at the mirror. Did Martine put it there on purpose to entertain her lovers? I suddenly wanted mirrors everywhere; I wanted to see sex from every angle. Looking back, I saw that Martine had stood up and unzipped her skirt, quickly dropping it on the floor to one side. She threw off her bra as she went over to the wardrobe that stood in the gloomiest corner of the room, and rustled around inside. When she turned back, I didn't know where to look first: at the bright silver barbells that pierced through both her nipples, or the enormous strap-on cock hanging from one hand.

She walked back and held it out. I took it in my hand, my eyes on stalks as I examined the huge contraption. It was molded with distended veins and the head was huge, engorged, as if it was about to explode. I ran my fingers around the edge of the head, imagining that rubbing against me, inside. My sex clenched.

"Wow," I murmured, looking up at Martine.

"You like it, huh?"

"It's um... amazing!"

"You must put it on."

"Me?" I blurted.

"Yes, I need more," she demanded, impatiently. The last round was obviously just for openers. I glanced at the clock; there was still time. Martine was already laid out on the bed, with her knees pulled up and her legs open. She had two fingers up to the hilt inside her sex, thrusting vigorously. Her breasts had rolled out to the sides. The piercings made her nipples look loaded, like twin torpedoes about to be launched. Between her legs, her fingers were slick with wetness.

I stood over her, filled with a sudden sense of longing and something else: power, raw power ebbing up from deep inside me. I hadn't worn a cock before. What would it be like? I felt a surge of vitality roar up inside me. I was going to fuck this woman, really fuck her. Hard. I stepped back and quickly climbed into the strap-on, pulling the holster tight against my pussy and between my buttocks. The thing felt heavy against my intimate parts, and outrageously large. I turned to glance at myself in the mirror, gasping when I saw it in profile. It looked totally strange and perverse in its size, brazen.

"I look obscene," I whispered to myself, a dart of sheer depravity flying around my veins.

58

Martine moaned from the bed, reaching out for me, her gaze on the cock. Christ, this was so hot! I knelt down between Martine's open legs and took a taste of her. She was so wet, and tasted so good, her nectar creamy and warm. She shuddered against my face while my tongue explored her. I had one hand on the cock, the other over one of her breasts. I captured the knotted skin between thumb and forefinger, rolling the steel barbell between my fingers. I was gratified to hear her moans growing louder. I lifted my head to suck on the other nipple, my tongue toying with the barbell while my hips moved between hers. Martine looked down when I whispered her name. I guided her hand over the huge head of the molded object, lubricating it with her wet fingers.

"Oh yes, now," Martine urged. I began to edge the massive head of the cock into the slippery entrance to her sex, angling my hips to ease the upright cock inside.

"Oh, *Mon Dieu*," Martine cried out.

I groaned. "Can you take more of it?"

"Yes!" As if to confirm it she grabbed the cock and hit a switch at its base. I gasped with shock when it started to vibrate, reverberating between us and sending a little jagged riff that went straight up into my clit.

Oh my!

I was wired, hugely aroused and totally empowered. I looked down at the woman spread in front of me, all wet with sex and wanting. She was like a pool of liquid lust on the bed, bubbling up, ready to be brought off. A sense of sheer and absolute power traversed my body. I pulled the base of the cock up against my clit with both hands, enjoying the weight and the vibrations there, where I was taut and pounding. The molded thing in my hands felt like a weapon and I jutted my hips forward, reaching and testing the tender succulent flesh of Martine's hole. I worked my hips slowly, edging it inside. Martine's

59

hands flew up to the metal bed frame to brace herself. She began to rock in turn with my thrusts

"Oh yes, push hard, " she mumbled. I lifted myself onto my arms, pushing the strap-on firmly against the resistance it met. She suddenly grabbed at my arms. Her hips bucked wildly. I leaned forward, watching the reflection of our bodies in the mirror, the line of my breasts heaving up as I moved back and forth between the other woman's thighs. It looked so hot. I was fucking her; I was fucking this hot glam-bitch with an enormous strap-on cock. My sex was on fire with arousal, the threat of another climax trembling right down into my hard-working thighs.

"Oh, Kim, I like you lots!" she cried out, gasps of pleasure and laughter escaping her. Her neck arched up, her eyelids lowering. She was so close.

"I like you lots too," I replied, grinning, loving her foreign tongue, and thrust hard. She reached down to the juncture of our bodies, rubbing her clit. The fingers of her free hand fastened over my nipple, pinching me while she bucked up. The pinch traversed my body, wiring itself into the heat between my thighs and I had to fight the urge to shout my pleasure aloud. I looked down at the bucking woman beneath me and grabbed the base of the cock, crushing my clit hard against it, sending us both right over the edge.

Non, je ne regrette rien. I hummed the old Edith Piaf number as I hauled my Land Rover into its bay in the underground car park at HQ and stepped out, grabbing my portfolio.

"Hey, Kim, how did it go?" Jack was waving over to me as he threw his briefcase into his Merc. I had caught him just before he left for the board meeting. What a bonus.

"Success. They went for the whole campaign, web slots and all." It was a massive contract for the company, my best work to date.

"Excellent, I knew you'd pull it off. That pay rise of yours is secure."

He saluted as he climbed into the car, and then stuck his head out of the window. "And you be sure you take yourself a good lunch break, you deserve it!"

I smiled to myself as I headed for the lift. *Too right, honey.* I had just enjoyed the best lunch break I'd ever had, and with a pay raise in the offing, I could afford to visit Kilpatrick's for lunch more often-just as Martine had suggested I should. Now - how was that for staff motivation?

UNLEASHED

THE IMPORTANCE OF GOOD NETWORKING

The importance of good networking became intimately apparent to me when I got to grips with Charlie Sedgemore, our new IT man. In fact Charlie hammered the fundamentals of good networking home with such exquisite attention to detail that I was thoroughly fascinated. It's his specialist subject, and the day he arrived in our offices he became mine.

Belinda informed me of his presence that first day. She walked back into our cube, leaned over my monitor and mouthed "fresh meat" at me, nodding her head over beyond the next cube.

Fresh meat? My radar was immediately up and tuning into nearby conversations. Our open-plan, cube divided office space was such that you could pick it up or tune it out at will. "Where?"

"Three cubes thataway. New IT bloke designated to our floor." A smug, knowing smile lifted her mouth as she turned back to her PC.

I didn't bother to hide my curiosity; Belinda had known me for five years. Geeky, intelligent guys really did it for me. I was busting to see this bloke and check out the 'fresh meat' for myself. I ran my fingers through my hair and stood up, glancing casually across the cubes as I did so. I could see Dave Chatham, the IT manager for the whole building, talking to someone, but alas the other person was sitting down. A full on reconnaissance mission was required. Snatching up the outgoing documents from my mail tray I shimmied my skirt straight, smoothing it over my hips, and headed out of our cube.

Dave's head swiveled as I approached and I smiled over the cube wall, my glance going to the other guy. He had shaggy, black hair, long to his neck and unruly. He wore glasses with thin black frames. Deliciously geeky. He'd made an effort with his appearance, but he was barely passable for a business environment. I could see the creases in his brand new shirt. His tie wasn't quite done up properly. Lean and uncomfortable in his office clothes, my guess was he was fresh out of college. When I got to the entrance to his cube, I dropped my mail on the floor.

Both Dave and the new guy turned to watch as I bent to retrieve the envelopes. The new guy was riveted. He pushed his glasses up the bridge of his nose, revealing a wrist wound with thin, black leather twines-he had a bit of an alternative edge, perhaps? I had a sudden image of him playing guitar. As I stood up I rearranged my clothes and smiled over at the pair of them, apologizing for interrupting. That's how I got my introduction.

I soon learned more about Charlie. He was single, fresh out of college as I had thought, and a real computer whiz in both software and hardware. He knew computer systems inside out and, apparently, what this bloke didn't know about computer networks wasn't worth knowing. That information came from the more explicit networking resource of the office-gossip.

So I decided to go after him. No guarantees he would bite, but I was reasonably presentable and it sure as hell livens up the job trying. He was attractive in a subtle, bohemian way and the thought of getting to him turned me on. Part of it was the intelligence; part of it was the sexual thrill of coming onto him. It's the look of shock, the complete look of awe that this type of man gives when they are presented with a dominant woman in their space.

When I had the chance to chat with him by the coffee machine, I asked him if he would explain networking to me. "Just as a personal favor," I added, smiling. Of course I knew about networking, I had a taste for this kind of man, after all. No, something about listening to a bloke speak enthusiastically on the virtues of his chosen field gets me sexually aroused.

"Sure thing," he replied. He looked surprised but launched into his area of expertise with ease. I listened to him talking about harnessing the individual power of an intelligent unit and realizing the power of teamwork in computer terms, and my body was humming. Between my thighs, I was getting hotter all the time. There'd been two other men like this in my life, a French exchange student I met at college who could talk about metaphysics all night long, and a guy I'd dated for a year while he'd talked about software design. Both were intense, intelligent men. Like Charlie. Watching Charlie's green eyes flicker as he talked, I noticed how long his fingers were, wrapped around his coffee cup, how stark his cheekbones. I wanted to feed him. I wanted to fuck him.

"At the present time, the ultimate network is the Internet," he continued, "but who knows what the future holds." His eyes glittered with enthusiasm.

I set my coffee cup down and fanned myself lightly with the printed report in my hand.

"Sorry," he said, noticing me shifting from one foot to the other. "That's a bit technical and probably not what you meant." He was definitely the kind of man I went for, geeky, and not quite sure of himself outside his chosen field. I wanted to be the one to make him sure.

"That's exactly what I meant. Thanks Charlie. I hope you don't mind me asking, but do you play guitar?"

He looked surprised. "Yes, how did you know?"

I reached out and touched his fingers where they were wrapped around his coffee cup. "Your hands." Electricity raced between us. The surface of the coffee rippled, tension beading up in the cup. "I hope we get to chat again soon, I enjoyed it."

65

"Yes, that would be good," he said, pushing his glasses up the bridge of his nose with his free hand. I glanced back as I walked away and noticed that he was admiring my stacked heels. I made a mental note of that.

I plotted my moves and waited until Belinda was away for a training day and I had the cube to myself. I'd planned in advance, wore a low-cut top, short skirt, my highest heels and my sexiest underwear to give me confidence.

His eyes nearly popped out of their sockets when I appeared at his cube wall. I rested my elbows on it, leaning my boobs on top of the ledge. "Hi, Charlie. I hope I'm not interrupting. I've got a problem with my mouse."

I could tell he was trying desperately to prize his gaze away from my chest area. Smiling, I leaned further forward, my boobs spilling out of my top. "Do I have to fill in a form to get your attention?"

"No, definitely not." He grinned and clutched at the edge of his desk as he stood up. "It probably just needs a new part. I'll check it out now."

Perfect.

He followed close behind me and as we wended our way back to my cube I felt his eyes boring into me. I gestured at the desk. He sat in my chair. I put my hands on his shoulders, stood behind him and peered at the computer alongside him. I could feel his shoulders grow taut under my hands. The sexual tension was stacking up with every moment. He blinked several times before continuing. He was a loaded weapon about to blow.

Wriggling the mouse, he shook his head. "Yup, it's dead. I've got a batch of spares back in my cube. I'll fetch one now." Reluctantly, he stood up, one finger adjusting his collar as he glanced over me again.

Oh, the sweet combination of arousal and discomfort was too good. "You're the expert, but I should probably mention it happened before and Belinda found the connector had dislodged." This time I'd ensured that the connector had dislodged. "Maybe you should check that first?"

"I guess I should," he replied, while his eyes dropped to the floor. He was staring at my shoes and feet in a kind of mesmerized trance.

After a moment, I gestured under the desk with a smile. He got down on his hands and knees, giving me a look at his tight buttocks. Nice. When he crawled under the desk, I sat back down in the chair, trapping him in there.

Leaning down, I flashed him an eyeful of cleavage. "Take your time," I murmured.

He shuffled around and his whole body jolted when he caught sight of me. His head whacked the underside of the desk and it shuddered. "Shit. I mean, sorry."

I bit my lip, containing my urge to chuckle. "Is it okay if I sit here while you are underneath?"

"Yes. Please do."

I sat back, easing the chair in and shifting my legs nearer him. Even through my stockings, I could feel his breath hot on my skin. I had got him well and truly trapped. Rubbing one calf with the toe of the other foot, I noticed that it was very quiet under there. It was working. I moved my legs into different positions, sometimes brushing against him. Not a sound or a move came from underneath the desk, but the intense heat welling from under there was the signal I needed. Taking a deep breath, I pushed my swivel chair back, lifted one stacked heel up and pivoted it on the edge of my desk, flashing the underside of my thigh and stocking tops at him.

He was scrunched in the same position, his eyes glazed as he stared up at me in disbelief. He didn't look like he was trying to go anywhere in a hurry, in fact he hadn't budged since I'd sat down.

My pulse was racing. "Is it okay down there for you, Charlie?"

He gave a hoarse laugh. "Yes, I'm um, just admiring the view."

Brave. And now that he'd bitten, it was all systems go. Our very own network was up and running. "You can touch me if you want to." I could hear voices in the distance outside the cube, but they were fast zoning out, my attention fully harnessed.

With hardly a second's hesitation, one hand reached for me, but it was the foot still on the floor he went for. Stroking it with his fingers, he moved slowly over it, then under its arch and around its heel. With tentative fingers, he stroked the top of my foot with such adoration, that my head drop back and my hands gripped the arms of my chair. I'd hit gold! The man was a pure sensualist. He slipped his fingers around the back of my ankle and lowered his head to kiss the toe of my shoe. What a rush! Sensation shot the length of my leg; my pussy prickled with anxiety, needy for contact. I had to hold tight to stop from squirming in my seat.

He ran his mouth up my shin, and then kissed my knee. Using both hands, he stroked my inner thighs, reverently embracing my stocking tops. I was starting to tremble. Tension and need thrummed just inches from his hands, and he was closing. I watched the glossy surface of his hair as he moved in. He stroked one finger down the surface of my panties, pushing it into the groove of my pussy, tantalizing my clit. I gasped aloud. My foot skidded against the desk, my right leg twitched and bounced against him. I was about to urge him on, desperately, when he snuck a finger down one side of the fabric and thrust it underneath.

I heard him groan and saw him shuffle, and then I grew light-headed when he moved the pad of his finger into my groove, more fingertips following. My eyes clamped shut. He paddled his fingers against me, maddening my clit and the sensitive folds surrounding it. The contact was too good. My hips were rolling into him and he worked me harder, each of his fingers moving independently. *Like strumming a guitar.* The thought echoed through my mind as a sweet, sudden orgasm hit me.

I heard his voice in the distance. Opening my eyes, I saw him smiling up at me from between my open legs. "I said I better get back to my desk now, but, um, perhaps we could go for a drink after work?"

I pulled myself together. "Yes, I'd love to go for a drink. I have to work until six, why don't I come over to you when I'm done?" An idea was already ticking over in my mind. "Could you plug my mouse back in before you go." I winked.

He stared at me for several moments until recognition registered in his expression. "You did that to get me down here?"

"It was all that talk about networking." I could tell he thought I was joking. Little did he know.

He ducked back under the desk and I stood up from the chair, letting him emerge without further hindrance. As he did, he adjusted the bulge in his pants.

I snatched at his wrist, holding his hand on his cock. "I'll help you with that when I come over to your cube, later." I wanted to see what he had in his pants soon; we could go for the drink afterwards.

"I can hardly wait," he replied, pushing his glasses up his nose with his free hand. His eyes were glazed; he was in a bad way.

Power rushed in my veins. "I'll send you a message every hour from now until then, just to be sure that you don't forget I'm coming."

His eyes flashed shut. I felt his hand tighten on his cock. I moved away when I heard voices passing and he grabbed a file to cover his crotch-practical and quick-witted too.

Once an hour I sent him a message, questioning him about male-to-female connectors and spare parts. His replies assured me he would be pleased to look into any needs I had as soon as humanly possible. I couldn't help touching myself under the desk, thrilled that my scheme had worked. My pussy was heavy and sensitive from the orgasm he'd given me, my cunt aching for more. He was good with his hands, his attention to feet and shoes an unexpected bonus. Each time I sent him a mail I thanked him for his kind attentions and told him how much it was appreciated. I felt his responses in his words, coming over the network and in the atmosphere across the office. The clock ticked on, arousal building with every moment.

At five past six, the only other person around was the cleaner who was vacuuming each cube starting on the far side. I shut down my documents, grabbed my bag and headed over to Charlie's cube.

He grinned when I leaned over the wall. "Hello," he said and eased his chair out from the desk.

I stared pointedly at his crotch then sidled into the cube. "We're all alone here apart from the cleaner. She won't get over here for ages." I bent over him, my hands on the arms of his chair, trapping him in it, and kissed him on the mouth. His body was rigid and he moaned under me. "I've been hot for more ever since this morning," I said as I pulled back. Glancing down at his crotch I could see that his bulge had got bigger. Reaching for his belt I looked him in the eye. "I want to sit on your cock."

I thought his eyes would pop out of his head. He about managed to nod, fumbling with his fly, helping me. His dick bounced out. "I've been hard most of the afternoon," he muttered. "Seeing you come, earlier," he added, as if he needed an explanation.

I leaned over him and then reached for the condom packet I'd tucked into my cleavage.

"Man, that is so hot." He groaned as I pulled it out.

"I thought you might like it." I chuckled and then bent to run my tongue over the head of his cock. He shuddered vigorously, his hands clutching at the arms of his chair. I rolled the condom down the length of him. "I'm going to grind your cock until you come, right here and right now."

He gave a soft, disbelieving laugh, lifting his hands in the air nonchalantly before clutching at the arms of the chair again. "Feel free."

I pulled my skirt up and he stared, wide-eyed. I'd taken my panties off this time. I turned around, forced his legs shut with my knees, straddling them, my skirt up around my waist. Behind me I heard him cursing under his breath.

"Oh, I'm doing this on one condition,"" I said over my shoulder. "You've got to talk dirty to me."

The look on his face was priceless. "Dirty?"

I nodded. "Tell me about networks again, Charlie. Tell me about plugging into the central supply, tell me about system routing." I winked over my shoulder and lowered myself down, guiding his cock inside me.

"That's so good." He moaned as I drove myself down on to him. Each time I lifted up higher to thrust deeper again, I could see the cleaner on the far side of the office going about her business, oblivious to what we were up to. Ah, the network of intrigue that can exist in open plan offices.

"Tell me, Charlie."

"Jesus, I thought you were kidding."

I squeezed his cock tight, grinding my hips. "Oh no, I wasn't kidding. It really turns me on."

"Networking is essential...for a company to function at...full capacity." He staggered his way through the sentence, his fingers biting into my buttocks.

"Oh that's good." Leaning forward, I clutched the edge of his desk and then began to pump. His cock felt good, rock-hard and burning hot from waiting. I rode it, squeezing it tight and milking every drop of pleasure out of him. "Go on."

"It maximizes return, by using all available...power...resources as and when needed."

When I lifted up, he moaned behind me mumbling something about how good it looked. My cunt started melting and my knuckles went white as I gripped onto the table.

"Key basic factors include..." He groaned. "...accurate server configuration."

I was close to coming, and then I noticed movement in the periphery of my vision. "The cleaner's on her way over, hurry," I blurted, anxiety hitting me. We were both so close, I didn't even know if I could stop. I didn't have to think about it for long, because suddenly my view shifted and my feet left the floor. Charlie shoved me bodily over his desk. My breasts were crushed on the surface, my hands clutching at handfuls of paperwork, bits of hard drive and other computer gear on the desk as I grappled for purchase.

He leaned over my back; his cock still wedged deep and getting deeper still as he banged into me. "A solid, working network ensures no loss of packets in transfer," he said against my ear, with a hoarse laugh.

That was too good! My cunt was on fire. My cervix crushed and throbbing. I moaned, bit on my wrist as I came, my body spasming uncontrollably, release flooding me. "Do you think this network is secure enough?" I urged him on to his completion, my lips drawn back as hot wave upon wave of pleasure shot through my cunt.

"We're about to find out." He wedged deep, lifting my hips from the desk, and shot his load.

With a show of efficiency and nonchalance that stunned me, he rocked back into the chair, lifting me bodily to my feet, and pulled my skirt down around my hips. By the time the cleaner appeared by his cube, he'd zipped up, straightened my skirt and was leading me through a network directory on his screen.

"Good networking is the key to quality IT systems. An international organization such as ours would be useless without one." He waved at the cleaner as she passed by and then stopped me swaying with one hand. "Now, how about that drink?"

I nodded, laughing, and rested against the edge of the desk to steady myself. I needed that drink, just like I needed a good IT man. I leaned over and kissed him on the mouth, my fingers meshing in his hair. I savored that kiss, and so did he, meeting it openly, his tongue tasting me slowly, reverently.

"Can we do this again?" I asked when we drew back.

He nodded and slipped his hand between my thighs, stroked my damp flesh, applying pressure in all the right places. His thumb resting on my over-sensitive clit was too good. "A good network needs regular maintenance," he replied, one eyebrow lifting.

I think I fell in love with him in that moment. "In that case, it's a good job I've found me such an expert," I replied, and pulled him into my arms.

UNLEASHED

SASKIA WALKER

KEEPING TIME

Watching the Maestro in action always got me hot. We'd been working it for nearly two hours and the heat between my thighs had been building by the second. I ached to lift my hair from the back of my neck, to squeeze my thighs together, to put my hands into my underwear and crush my pussy in my fingers. Even my clarinet felt hot in my hands and I squirmed on my seat, trying to focus.

It was something about the way he looked, so intense and focused, while he stood on the podium in front of us, leading his musicians through the score. He exuded an aura of power, more than any other conductor I had worked with, and it had me at meltdown point. His hair flashed back from his forehead and then his roving eyes suddenly met mine. I looked away, trying to concentrate on my sheet music.

Too late.

"Enough." He slammed his baton down on the podium and stepped down from it, pacing toward us. "Some of you are letting your concentration wander." His steady gaze did a slow circuit of the orchestra and several people shuffled in their seats. My breath was trapped in my lungs. He paused when he reached me. "Let's call it a day." A hum of appreciation went around the assembled musicians. "Except for Caroline and Jeremy," he added, "the rest of you can go."

I glanced over at Jeremy, who sighed and reached for his violin case. He was losing it because they had a new baby at home and he was justifiably tired-what was my excuse? We had a performance in two days and I was

75

letting deviant thoughts about the Maestro distract me from our penultimate rehearsal.

By the time I'd packed up my clarinet and sheet music he'd had a quiet word with Jeremy. Jeremy gave me a wave and a sympathetic smile, and then followed the last few musicians who were exiting from the stage.

The Maestro paced back and forth, waiting for me. I walked over to him and set my clarinet case down by my feet. As I did I noticed that his fine linen shirt was open at the collar, revealing the strong column of his neck, and that his black evening jacket failed to mask the breadth of his shoulders. Folding my hands in front of me, I obediently waited to see what he would say to me.

He waited until the last figure disappeared through the door and it swung closed, leaving us alone together in the auditorium. There was an eerie, tense silence surrounding us. It only broke when he stepped forward and his heels sounded against the floor of the stage. He looked me up and down, his stare determined and keen. I could feel the weight of it through my shirt and my pulse tripped higher. With one finger, he reached out and trailed down the buttons of my shirt.

"Caroline, if Stravinsky were here he'd be appalled by your behavior during our rendition of this masterpiece." The back of his hand made brief and tantalizing contact with my breasts, where I ached for more. "Do I have to drum into you the importance of giving it your full concentration?"

"Forgive me," I murmured, "I was distracted." The problem was that I got even hotter when he was in the mood to chastise; he looked demonic, and I was his willing slave. My heart was pounding. I looked at him pleadingly from under my lashes. I was so sexually aroused, I couldn't help myself.

"You're a dirty girl thinking dirty thoughts, it's written all over your face... and when your mind drifts, you distract others...namely me!" A frown marked his brow, but I could see the black lust in his eyes. "You're in heat, and with that damn clarinet in your mouth I warrant you make half the orchestra want you." He snatched up his baton from the podium. "I think you'll agree that some basic training in focusing on the job is in order." His voice was more subdued, but he was simmering with barely contained sexual tension, just as I was.

I managed to nod.

He held the baton between his hands, testing its subtle power, and then pointed it at the podium. "Kneel," he instructed. .

"Yes, Maestro." I hurried toward the step where he usually stood and knelt down on it.

"Bend over."

I did as instructed, my hair falling forward, casting my face in darkness.

"Imagine how you'd feel if there were a full house out there, watching you, knowing you were a horny little slut who had to be reprimanded for your lack of self control."

I glanced back to where the empty rows of stalls were visible in the semi-gloom, but I could almost feel the audience's eyes on me, I could hear their muffled gasps as he lifted my skirt with his baton, revealing my stockings and my black lace panties. He kept pushing the skirt up until it gathered around my waist.

I groaned, my fingers gripping tight to the base of the podium.

"Do you want to be humiliated like this?"

Oh, but he knew I did.

"I want you," I blurted, unable to hold back the words.

He paused, and I could feel the tension in him. "All in good time," he murmured, and his voice was hoarse with restraint. "We have to work this out of your system; you know that, don't you?"

The baton followed the line of my slit, poking the fabric in against my swollen, sensitive folds until he reached my clit. When he touched me there, prodding firmly, I nodded, my head hanging down, my hair trailing the floor.

"Pull down your panties and let me see you."

I swallowed hard and wriggled my damp underwear down my thighs until it fell around my knees.

"You must learn to concentrate on keeping time, no matter what sort of distraction is going on, is that clear?"

Again, I nodded. He knew this would be difficult for me.

"Stravinsky accents the notes that are off beat," he continued. "I will mark the tempo on your delectable derrière, and you will anticipate the change of tempo that occurs in the piece you were just playing."

I squeezed my eyes shut, wondering how I'd ever manage it. The driving beats, the pulsating rhythm-but with me as his instrument!

"Is that understood?"

"Yes, Maestro."

Without further ado, he got into position and the baton made quick bursts of contact on my buttocks. The sting and the suddenness of it made me shudder. Heat speared from the points of contact, as if each strike connected with the pounding pulse that had been raging inside me. Pleasure, pain and shame quickly engulfed me, swamping me with a new, fierce wave of desire. But I had to concentrate; he was following the music precisely, the flick of his wrist building the rhythm toward the important shift. I arched my back, anticipating the quaver note.

It was coming. "Now," I cried.

"Good girl, very good." He paused

78

While he toyed with his baton and admired his handiwork, the heat spread out from my buttocks, heightening the points of arousal in my body, each sting fuelling the need for more physical contact. I shuffled on my hands and knees; my breasts were tight and restricted within my orchestra uniform blouse, pounding with sensation, the nipples hard against the fabric. My thighs were damp; I could smell my own desire mounting all around us. I felt the baton move lower, drawing a line across the sensitive flesh at the top of my thighs.

"Your pale skin marks in the most spectacular way, my dear," he commented.

I knew. I felt it, burning hot and pulsating.

"Right, one more time, for good measure."

I sucked in my breath and got ready to count again. The baton flicked against the underside of my buttocks, in the sensitive niche at the top of my thighs, making brief, maddening contact with my pussy. I bit my lip to hold back from moaning my reaction out loud. Seconds later, when I called out the beat differentiation, the echo of my voice in the auditorium was much less strong this time.

I panted, my whole nether region aflame. I became aware of him moving and looked back at him. He was now holding a baton of a different kind. His cock, hard and ready for me, as I knew it would be. He knelt down behind me, pushing my legs farther apart with a demanding knee.

"I cannot believe it's my own wife that I have to bring to order for her concentration."

I glanced over my shoulder again. "At least it means you get to enjoy the punishment as well?" I offered.

He slapped me on the buttock and positioned my hips. "If I thought you'd done that on purpose for some attention, lady, you'd be in even bigger trouble," he muttered, reaching down to run a knowing thumb back and forth over my clit.

My body was so wired that I reached orgasm moments later, crying out with relief. I was still shuddering when he opened me up with two fingers and shoved his cock inside me, capturing me as I ebbed back from the edge, quickly sending me back to that glorious precipice again.

"Oh yes," I groaned in relief, suddenly filled with him, my whole innards melting with pleasure and clasping him gratefully. My core was red hot. From knees to waist my body was singing and my arms felt too weak to support me. He pulled my hips hard on to him, lifting me physically, his cock bruising up against my cervix. When his body moved against my scored buttocks it sent shock waves through me. I grasped at the podium for anchorage and rode each tortuous wave of pleasure, loving its brutal intensity.

And, yes, he knew that I had caught his eye on purpose, we both did. Besides, I never, ever, missed a beat. Keyed up and horny after each and every orchestra session, we had to make sweet music our own way. And it just so happened that I was the Maestro's favorite instrument-but I wouldn't have it any other way.

THE WOMAN IN HIS ROOM

Luke had a woman in his room.

I could hear the familiar sound of his voice-gravely and seductive-as it filtered out of the partly open bedroom door. I paused on the landing and listened. There was music playing in the background, something sensual and rhythmic. Then I heard the woman's laughter, and something inside me altered.

The small part of me that was still immature balked because it was some other woman, and not me. But the part of me that was a young woman who was becoming more deeply aware of her own sexuality-the part that had been stimulated by my exposure to Luke in our home-responded altogether differently.

Desire, and the sure knowledge of my own needs, flamed inside me. The crush I had been nurturing for Luke changed. It wasn't an ethereal emotion cloaked in sighs of longing and wistful glances anymore. It was hardcore lust. And I liked it.

I liked this feeling of being a woman who had physical needs that were more powerful than her daydreams. I could just as easily be that woman in Luke's room. I wanted to be that woman, it was as simple as that.

I'd wanted Luke since the day he had moved in, three weeks earlier. I doubt my father would have let his business partner stay over after his wife threw him out, had he known that I would develop an obsession with him. Dad thought I was far too busy at college. Too busy to notice a man like Luke? No way.

"You've met Luke, haven't you, Karen?" my dad had said when Luke walked into our house that first night, a suit carrier flung casually over one shoulder, an overnight

81

bag in the other hand. I remember being glued to the spot, thinking that I'd surely remembered him if I'd met him before. Apparently I had, briefly. Four years earlier. I guess I'd been different then. I'd been fifteen and a tomboy. Now I was at college, and my focus was on the adult world, with all its risks and discoveries.

Luke had set down the bag he held and put his hand out to me. "You've grown up," he said under his breath and looked at me with an appraising stare that made me feel hot all over.

I managed to put my hand in his. He held it tightly, drawing me closer in against him. I looked up into his wickedly suggestive eyes, and it made my pussy clench.

My mother disapproved of him. Why had his wife thrown him out? she demanded of my dad, when Luke was out of the house. Dad wouldn't answer. I made up my own reasons, fantasies that featured me in a starring role. Maybe he left his wife for a hot younger woman, me. The truth was that Luke moving in had made something shift in my world. He was a man, a real man. Sex with him wouldn't be like the fumbling bad sex I'd had with a guy I met at college. As soon as I saw Luke, I knew that it wouldn't feel like that, not with him. Sex would be exciting, maybe even kinky. The idea of it fascinated me.

Luke wasn't what you'd call handsome, but he was attractive in a bad boy sort of a way. Tall and leanly muscled, his body suggested athletic vigor. His features were craggy, his hair cut close to his head. He had a maverick quality about him that appealed to the dark side of my imagination. At night I'd lay in my bed and I'd imagine there was no wall between our rooms and that I could reach out and touch his body. I'd imagine him responding. He'd climb over me and screw me into the bed, teaching me what it was like to be fucked by a real man.

During the day when he was out I would go into his room and touch his things. Sometimes I even lay down on his bed. I would close my eyes and breath him in, getting high on the smell of his body and his expensive cologne, the experience building up a frenzy of longing inside me. What if he walked in and found me there? The idea of being caught by him made it even worse. Sometimes I'd push my hand inside my jeans and press my panties into the seam of my pussy, massaging my clit for relief.

Then my parents went away for a fortnight, leaving me in Luke's care. Oh, the irony. If only they had known how much the idea of it excited me.

It was our first night alone, and I had been thinking about him all evening, barely aware of the blockbuster movie I'd gone to see with my friends. I wanted to get home, to see if Luke was there.

But now he had a woman in there with him, and that woman wasn't me.

I was intensely curious, and it struck me that I was getting hot just thinking about him having sex; even if it wasn't me he was having it with. The push-pull reaction of the unexpected situation had me on edge. Torn, I glanced at my bedroom door. He probably thought I was in there, asleep. Like a good girl. I looked back at his door, and saw a shadow move across the room beyond.

His shadow.

I couldn't walk away.

Luckily I hadn't switched the landing light on. I was glad of the darkness, glad that I was standing in the gloom and that his door was open and I could see into his room. I'd had a couple of beers earlier. That probably helped, too. I stepped farther along the landing, until I could see him.

He had his shirt off. I'd seen him semi-naked before, in the kitchen in the mornings. He'd have a towel round his waist, his body still damp and gleaming from the shower. I managed to muster up an early morning conversation so I could watch him pouring out coffee, stirring in three teaspoons of sugar as he chatted to me easily, watching me all the while. Watching me in a way that made my body feel womanly and alive. That's what he'd done to me; he'd made me feel alive. And although I remember saying something in response to his early morning conversations, it wasn't what I was thinking. What I was thinking was X-rated. I wanted him to bend me over the breakfast bar and introduce me to real sex.

The woman was sitting back on his bed, and he had his knees pressed against hers. As I watched, he bent over her and pushed her silky red dress up along her thigh, exposing her panties. Craning my neck, I could see that they were very small, a narrow strip of sheer black fabric. Luke stroked the front of them, and when he did her hips moved on the bed, rocking and lifting under his touch.

My pussy ached to be stroked that way. My pulse was racing. Would he strip? Would I see him naked, as I longed to do?

He spoke to her in a low voice. I couldn't hear what he said. Then he straightened up and she also moved, into an upright sitting position. The light was obscured and before I knew what was happening the door opened wide and Luke's shape filled the frame, a dark silhouette against the light behind him.

My hand went to my throat, but there was no time to try to escape.

"Well, hello," he said. He didn't sound surprised. Did he know I'd been there, watching?

"I was at the cinema, just got back." I could hear my own breathlessness. The light was behind him, but I could see that his fly was open, the belt on his jeans dangling suggestively down his thigh.

"I knew you were out here, Karen," he said more quietly. "I heard you come in. I was waiting for you to get back."

I stared at him in stunned silence. He knew I was here. He knew...he knew I wanted to go into his room and be with him, that was what he was insinuating. I could hear it in his tone. Did he know I'd already been in there, on his bed? I could feel my face growing hot.

He pushed the door wide open. The woman was sitting on the bed looking in my direction with a curious expression. Perhaps it mirrored my own. Even from here I could see she was pretty. She had jet-black hair and a smile hovered around her ruby painted lips.

"Come in, join the party," Luke said. The casual remark was powerfully suggestive. It went right through me, thrilling every ounce of me. He lifted his hand. He was holding a glass, and I heard ice chink as he shifted it from side to side invitingly. "You know you want to."

I did want to. That's the moment I addressed what was inside me, what I was becoming-a woman who could be proactive about her desires. I had a choice, but I knew what I wanted, and he'd invited me closer to it. I stepped past him and into the room, my entire skin racing.

Tension beaded up my spine when I heard him close the door. He stood at my back. I had to force myself to breathe, telling myself over and over to chill.

The woman sitting on the bed ran her fingers through her hair as she looked me over, her body moving in time with the music. "You're even prettier than Luke said you were."

She knew about me? That was when it hit home. He had planned this; he'd told her about me. Should I be annoyed? I looked at her more closely. She was maybe a couple of years older than me but she had an edge, a self-assured confidence I knew I didn't have, but wanted.

She patted the bed beside her, and when I sat down, she lifted a tumbler from the floor and offered it to me.

Luke followed and stood close by, at the foot of the bed. When I glanced his way, I got an eyeful of bare chest and open fly. Just what I wanted. The only part I wasn't sure about was the other woman.

"I'm Lisa," she said. "I'm glad you came to play with us?"

She was flirting with me.

I didn't think it was possible for my temperature to rise any more than it already had, but it did. Okay. We were going to "play," and I didn't think she was referring to a card game. She was looking at me as if she were deciding which item of my clothing to take off first. Luke, half undressed already, smiled down at us. I was getting the gist of the setup now. He wanted two women. As long as one of them was me, I figured I could roll with it.

But the way she was looking at me?that did weird things to me. She was very sexy. I found I wanted her to flirt with me some more. I swigged heavily from the glass. It was whiskey. The potent liquid washed over my tongue and, when I swallowed, the hit was just what I needed. "Thanks," I said as I handed the glass back, and tried to look as relaxed as she did. Crossing my legs, I rested one hand on the surface of the bed.

Luke smiled down at me, approvingly. I had to take a deep breath to stop myself from grinning like an idiot. Jesus, this was really happening. All I could think was: Thank god for the whiskey.

The woman, Lisa, sprawled easily onto the bed beside me. When she got settled she reached over and ran her hand down the length of my hair. I stared at her, and when she paused with her fingers close against my neck, I smiled. She moved lower, touching my breasts briefly through my T-shirt, before wrapping her arm around my waist and drawing me closer to her.

I rolled onto the bed next to her and she kissed me full on the mouth. I was stunned, and stiffened. I'd never kissed another woman before. But then I melted, because she was all soft and yet full on, at the same time. I felt the urge to answer her, and I kissed her back.

Oh, how delicious that was. For a moment I almost forgot that Luke was there. Almost. When I looked back, he had a gleam in his eyes and the bulge at his groin was larger. Between my thighs I was aching with longing, and with him looming over the pair of us I felt the urge to be wild, to explore. I pushed my hand into Lisa's silky hair, and drew her in for another sweet kiss.

"Oh yeah, you're delicious," she said approvingly as we drew apart, pushing me over onto my back. She laughed gleefully, and it was infectious.

I bit my lip, but couldn't contain a giggle.

"You're really horny, aren't you?" She pulled my T-shirt up over my breasts and off, as she asked the question, then squeezed my nipples through my bra.

"I don't suppose there's any point in denying it," I responded, another laugh escaping my mouth when she shoved my bra to one side to tug on my nipple.

Before I knew what was happening, she had my sandals off, and my jeans undone. She wrenched them down my hips. Playfully, she lifted my panties and put her hand underneath them, touching my pussy. She watched my face for my reactions. My breath was captured in my chest. I glanced at Luke, who was looming close by. He looked as if he was about to pounce. I couldn't predict what was going to happen next, and that thrilled me.

When I didn't resist her, Lisa pulled the panties off of me as well. Luke looked me up and down. I lifted my arm and drew it over my face, closing my eyes, unable to watch him staring down at me when Lisa moved between my thighs.

I'm doing this with a woman, and Luke is watching. I felt slightly crazy, lack of control and sheer horniness sending me dizzy with pleasure. And then I felt her mouth close over my clit, and every nerve ending in my body roared approval.

Her tongue moved with purpose, tracing a pattern up and down over my clit, driving me mad. Her hands were locked around the top of my legs, her thumbs stroking the sensitive skin on the inside of my thighs in time with the movements of her clever tongue. This was alien to me, to have a woman seduce me, but it felt so fucking good and I didn't want her to stop. My head rolled from side to side on the bed, and I cried out loud, unable to keep it inside. "Oh, oh fuck, it's so good."

She knew just what to do, and when I was thoroughly wound up, she nudged at my clit with the tip of her tongue until I came, my body writhing as I spasmed and fluid ran down between my buttocks.

She rose up to her knees on the bed, and then she pulled her dress off in one long slow move. She was naked beneath, aside from that tiny G-string that barely covered her shaved pussy. She was sleek and lissome. Her breasts were small and pert, nipples hard and dark. Tossing her hair back, she looked down at me. "Fuck her now, Luke. She's so ready."

My face burned up, but she was right, boy, was she right. I shot a glance at him to see his reaction to her comment. He nodded at me when he saw me looking his way, and when he did, I clenched inside, my gaze automatically dropping to his groin. He undid the final two buttons on his fly. His cock jutted out from his hips, hard and ready. Holding it in an easy grip, he reached into his pocket with his free hand and pulled out a condom packet.

My hands were shaking, I knew they were, and I pressed them down onto the bed to keep them steady. I couldn't stop myself. He really did mean to use the condom on me. I stared at him rolling the rubber onto the hard shaft of his cock.

Lisa had moved to one side and was watching expectantly.

I could scarcely believe it. The surprise must have been there on my face, because Lisa chuckled softly and reached in to kiss me again, easing me back down on the bed. When I was flat against it, her hands roved over my breasts, and then she captured one nipple between finger and thumb, tweaking it. As I glanced down, I saw that her other hand was in between her thighs, where she was stroking herself.

"I like to watch, it makes me hot," she whispered. She flashed her eyes at me, and then her mouth closed over my other nipple, her teeth grazing it.

Tension ratcheted through me. My eyes closed, my legs falling open, and then I felt the weight of him, right there between my thighs, his hard erection pushing against me.

"Ready for me?" he asked, when my eyes flashed open and I looked at him. He was lifting my buttocks in his hands, maneuvering me into position, his cock already easing inside.

I managed to nod. I was so slick from Lisa's attention that he claimed me in one easy thrust, the head of his cock wedging up against my cervix. I moaned aloud and my body closed around him, gripping his hardness in relief. Pleasure rolled through me when he drew back and then thrust again.

Lisa was sucking hard on my breast and the pleasure arced through me to my core, where Luke was riding me hard, massaging the very quick of me with his cock. My orgasm was coming fast. I panted, hard. I

89

reached out, gripped onto his arm when wave after wave of pleasure hit me.

"Oh yes," he said, and thrust deep, staying there, while his cock jerked, sending an aftershock of pleasure through my sensitive cervix that made me cry out.

It took a full minute for me to catch my breath.

Lisa was snuggled up against my side, and she kissed my shoulder affectionately when Luke went to the bathroom.

"What about you?" I said, without thinking, brushing her hair out of her eyes.

"I'll get mine." She smiled. "Don't you worry about that." She winked at me.

"How you doing?" Luke asked as he rejoined us, lying on the opposite side of me to Lisa. He cupped my buttock with one hand as he asked the question, and smiled that wicked smile of his.

A breathless laugh escaped me. He knew just how well I was doing.

"Good, I'm doing good." I returned his smile, and then glanced over my shoulder at Lisa to include her. She made me curious. That hadn't gone away.

"I meant to tell you," Luke added, "I'll be moving out when your parents get back."

My hands tightened on his shoulder, and my smile faded. I didn't want hear that.

He squeezed my buttock tighter. "You'll have to come round and visit me in my new apartment."

I nodded, quickly.

"Both of you," he added.

At my back, Lisa chuckled softly. I felt her breath on my shoulder. Soft, seductive, and warm. She moved to spoon me, her hand stroking my side affectionately. I had her-so alluringly feminine-on one side of me, and Luke on the other-hard, hot, demanding and all man. Something joyous and liberated reveled in the decadence of it, the blatant mutual pleasure.

"I'm up for it," Lisa said, as she clambered over me, pushing Luke down on the bed and straddling his hips. "What about now. Ready for more?"

"Too right." He reached for the bedside table and grabbed a box of condoms. When he did, she winked at me again.

Could I watch him with her? A small residual doubt ticked inside me, but I couldn't look away when she grabbed a condom packet off him, opened it and rolled it onto the stiff shaft of his cock. Mounting him, she put her hands on her hips, circling on the head of his cock. The crown pressed into her slit, and I watched, mesmerized, as it eased up inside her, splitting her pussy open before my eyes.

The sight was so hot that my hand went to my clit, and I thrummed it as I watched her riding him. A moment later Luke reached out to me, pulled me closer and kissed me, thrusting his tongue into my mouth. The doubts inside of me slipped away. I was being introduced to a world of sensuality and erotic possibility.

And I was ready, ready for all of it.

A HOOK AND A TWIST

"There's something about being tied up with rope that brings out the sex kitten in me," Lizzie commented, loudly, while spooning an impressive helping of creamy torte into her glossy, red moue.

Georgina folded her napkin, dabbed her mouth, and looked at her watch. She was about to leave, I could tell. Now don't get me wrong; Georgina isn't a prude, far from it. None of the three of us are shy, retiring types and Georgina has well and truly earned her "London Ladette" label. She's a man-eater of mega proportions; she just can't stand Lizzie's attention-seeking attitude. The fact that several occupants of the exclusive Covent Garden cafe had turned toward us would be enough to try Georgina's patience.

"Of course it has to be hand-made rope, and it has to be done with true style," Lizzie gushed, "and by a proper master." She wiped a dribble of cream from her chin and smiled down her nose at us, as if pleased to note she had the attention of her pupils. That rankled a bit, I have to admit, but I bit back my pride and returned her smile. You have to play dumb with Lizzie or she won't spill.

Georgina stood up, pulling on her coat, and announced that she would be late for a meeting if she didn't run for the tube. Me? I was hooked. Hell, I can suffer Lizzie's condescending attitude to find out some juicy tidbit. I'm always willing to consider new ways to stimulate my inner sex kitten, and whilst I had enjoyed sex-play with cuffs, belts, and scarves, the mention of hand-made rope fascinated me.

Regrettably, I have to inform you that Lizzie's gushing narrative didn't give me the low down on the rope. Instead, she wanted to impress me about her new bloke. She failed; he sounded more like an upper-class twit than "a proper master." But my curiosity had been baited and the image of bespoke rope had lodged itself in my mind. What was it like? Would it release my inner sex kitten to be bound in it? What would it feel like running through my fingers, assessing its power to restrain?

I did some research and located several sources for the material. I also discovered to my amusement that you could have it dyed to match other items in your sex assemblage. I even got some samples, and found that I especially liked the feeling of the hemp; its natural resilience and strength felt very sexy in my hands. I was interested, yes, but at first I couldn't find a playmate to explore my new fascination with. I mentioned it to two lovers, one of whom thought I was joking; the other thought I was a few sandwiches short of a picnic. No, it wasn't until Carl Sanderson walked into my life, several months later, that I had the opportunity to pursue the fascination for real.

Carl Sanderson was a management consultant who had been hired by the powers that be where I worked. He was the hatchet man, the man who would resolve time management issues with certain our staff. I should have known he'd be into power games. The man positively exuded power. He walked into our offices one Monday morning and told us in no uncertain terms that he'd reviewed the procedures and things were about to be "well and truly shaken up." Yeah, I was prepared to be shaken up, in more ways than one.

I slid my glasses down my nose and observed him taking charge. He was attractive, not in the classical, good-looking sort of a way. He was strong and presentable, yes, but it was more like he had an underlying aura of power. Was it that quality that appealed to me?

His expression had a constant weathered look. You know, he'd been around the block a few times and his frown looked as if it was welded on. Even when he broke into a disarming grin, the frown was still there, like a testament to his intensity. His eyes were a piercing blue, his hair a no-nonsense cut. Beneath the sleeves of his Savile Row shirts, I could see that his muscles were large and strong. Oh yes, Carl was every bit the veneered brute.

He walked from desk to desk in our open-plan offices, delivering snappy orders and tearing a strip off anyone who hadn't been performing to schedule. I was lucky, I had a ringside seat but I wasn't due for any flack. As the CAD assistant, I responded to the needs of the departments that were actually having the scheduling problems. And boy, did I enjoy watching Carl flex his muscles in the workspace. It was midsummer and steamy hot in the city; you know, sex was always on my mind. When he finally paced my way, I sat back in my chair and swiveled to face him.

"Megan Brody, now you don't appear to be on my list." He paused in front of my desk. He had a lopsided smile, very suggestive. "Shame," he added.

I gave him my best come-on smile and crossed my legs high on the thigh. "I could easily cause some trouble for you, if that's what you're after," I offered, hopefully.

"I'm quite sure you could," he replied, eyeing my bare legs where my wraparound skirt had fallen open when I moved. He winked as he sauntered off. We had connected. I couldn't be more pleased.

By lunchtime that first day, I was entertaining full-blown fantasies about him. By the Tuesday, I'd snagged him for after-work drinks. By Thursday, we went for a bite to eat and then he asked me back to his place.

Dinner was light, by necessity- the heat, and the distraction of bodies wanting a different kind of feeding. We hit a noodle bar, sat on stools in front of the steaming kitchens and drank bottles of iced Asahi in an attempt to keep cool. I quizzed him about his work. The noise level grew as the place filled. He increasingly leaned toward me to chat. The smell of his after shave and the musk of his body raced through my senses, dancing alongside the smells of food cooking and exotic spices. Every sentence was laden with double entendre, discussions about power interchange and snapping people out of their daily routine. But you don't want me to tell you about our conversation; you want me to get to the juicy part. You want to know about the rope and how I found out he was one to play with. Okay. He invited me home and we abandoned our food.

The air moved through the tube stations like a sirocco, a welcome breeze all the same. We stepped out by his riverside apartment block and a breath of air from the water gave my mind a moment of tingling clarity. It was short lived. It was a humid night, and his high-rise location only seemed to magnetize the heady atmosphere of the city.

He flicked on light switches as he walked inside, revealing a sparse bachelor pad with low leather sofas and a coffee table made out of a sheet of Perspex standing on stacked shot glasses. Cute, I thought. He leaned down to the stereo and flicked it on. Music sprang out, feeding background beats to me from every corner. I dropped my bag on a chair, smiled at him, and then stalked closer to him, my hands on my hips. His gaze roved over my little black dress, my heels, my thin, angular frame. The atmosphere between us was high with sexual tension.

He paused rather deliberately, as if to make sure I was watching, before hitting another switch. *What was this about?* A series of spotlights flashed on one by one in the far corner of the room, throwing into stark relief a gym area complete with weights bench, free weights, workout bars roving high on the wall and floor-to-ceiling mirrors. Imagine my surprise when the area was fully lit and I saw the giant skein of wine-colored rope in the corner, knotted to the wall-mounted bars and dangling to the floor. I glanced back at him and noticed he was watching me, subtly, but watching for my reactions.

Well, what do you know?

I strolled over, my stacked heels clacking on the polished floorboards. I felt very self aware, but why wouldn't I? We'd done more than enough flirting to flag up reciprocal interest. I'd taken his invitation to come into his space, and now I discovered he might be the perfect person with whom to explore my curiosity about rope. Besides, his eyes were boring into my back; my entire skin was taut with tension. He'd put himself and his toys on offer. It was up to me push things on; I could sense that. I supposed that I could choose to ignore the presence of the rope or I could give him a signal.

I didn't really have a choice, now did I? My curiosity had well and truly got the better of me. I stroked the rope with one tentative, curious hand. It wasn't hemp, like the samples I had enjoyed; it was synthetic, slicker and somehow stronger. I glanced back at Carl. The hatchet man; all rippling muscle and contained sexual energy.

"Is it dyed to match anything in particular?"

His eyebrows lifted, but he was smiling. "Ah, I can tell you're a connoisseur."

I had to turn away so he wouldn't see me smile to myself. "Just curious," I replied, running it through my fingers. How many willing victims had he bound with it, I wondered?

"The weights bench," he replied, indicating the bench that stood alone beneath a spotlight.

The color did coordinate. Dark reds; like wine, like blood. I had a sudden image of a naked, pale body; spread-eagled face-down over the vinyl bench, bound and trussed in the wine-colored rope, being fucked from behind. I glanced at him over the top of my glasses, and smiled.

He groaned. "I'm sure others have mentioned this, Megan, but the way you look over your glasses is such a turn-on."

Well, I knew some men had a thing about girls in glasses, but his remark still surprised me. Was that why he had responded so readily to my flirting?

"In fact, it makes you look strong. Powerful."

"Really?" I couldn't contain my surprise. Now there's a twist, I thought to myself. Is that what he wanted, for me to be the powerful one? I was thrilled. I loved sexual role-play and power interchange. How could I not totally love the idea of dominating a brute of a man like Carl? Arousal sped through my veins. My inner sex kitten was up and out, skidding across the floor with claws out, ready to pounce. I was well and truly interested now.

I unlatched the skein of rope from the bars and began to unwind it as I walked back toward him. When I drew up in front of him, he grasped the rope and tugged. I held tight. The rope went taut between us. He had a wild look in his eye. For a moment I wondered if he had changed his mind. Did he want to take control, after all? I reached for his head with my free hand and pulled him down for an open-mouthed kiss. He moaned into my mouth when I slid my tongue along the inside of his lower lip, very deliberately, sensitizing him and beckoning his tongue into my mouth. I was loading up my arsenal of domina tricks.

When I felt his hold on the rope slacken, I tugged. His body was against mine. Powerful, masculine: cocked and ready for action. I felt a surge of triumph. Oh yes, I was going to enjoy binding him up in his rope, gaining full control of his testosterone-fueled physique.

"I want to play, and I'd like you to strip," I murmured, as we pulled apart. I had said my thoughts aloud and almost jolted at the sound of my own voice. But my body was pulsing with arousal. I was on a roll. "I think we both know what's going on here, Carl, don't we?"

He nodded, his eyes bright with interest, his fingers quickly wending their way through his shirt buttons. He kicked off his shoes and abandoned his clothes.

"Sit here." I indicated the weights bench, while eyeing his body. My heart was racing; my focus closing in on bench, man, rope.

His eyes never left mine.

I reached over and locked the back support into the upright position, so that his upper body would be on an incline. His cock was rising before my eyes, his body rippling with movement. He was flexing his corded muscles, preparing for what was ahead. I had to drag my gaze away as he took his seat and I moved to stand behind him.

Arms first. I braced myself for action and threw the rope out across the floor, shaking out the loops. Snatching up one end, I squatted down behind him, pulled his wrists together and secured them inside a figure-eight knot. The rope coiled and twisted across the floor as I worked; alive and supple as a serpent.

He was watching me in the mirrors. "You're adept with knots," he commented and shook his head, disbelievingly, as if he'd made a real find. His expectations were now very high. My hands trembled slightly. I hoped I wasn't going to let him down! I silently ordered myself to go with the flow and follow my instincts.

"Blame the childhood holidays spent boating. My father was a fanatic."

"Oh, I'm not complaining."

I walked around him at that very moment and pulled the rope across his chest.

"Far from it," he added, as I began to truss him to the bench in true earnest.

His nipples were already hard. I wanted to see them trapped between two twists of rope. When I did exactly that, I thought he was going to raise the roof with his enthusiastic grunts.

"Fuck you're good," he muttered, his eyes going to the ceiling and husky laughter escaping from his lungs.

"Why thank you." I was loving every moment of his submission.

The humidity levels only seemed to rise by the moment. I was creaming, my thighs slick with sweat, my g-string clinging to the damp heat in my groin.

I wound the rope around his torso, across his hips and thighs, carefully arranging it either side of his cock, lifting his balls between the lines of rope to ensure a snug fit. He cursed under his breath, but I took a deep breath and didn't let it distract me from my purpose. When I had secured his ankles, tying him to the struts of the bench, I stood back to admire my handiwork.

What a sight!

His cock was dark with blood and distended to its limits, poking out demandingly between the ropes that contained him, the ropes that applied enough pressure to keep him on edge. His muscles seemed even stronger in their containment. His torso bowed under the rope, instinctively working against its enclosure. He was a gorgeous brute of a man, and I had him restrained.

Oh, it fast grew hotter under those spotlights, fast grew hotter when I stalked around him, admiring the sight from every angle, watching his growing anxiety with my hungry eyes. I stripped off my dress, my bra, and my G-string, kicking them across the floor. I kept on my stacked

100

heels because they made me feel powerful enough to take him on, and the glasses, as a concession for Carl.

It was then that I caught sight of myself in the floor-to-ceiling mirror. For a moment, I was shocked. The chic designer frames perched on my nose were the only nod to socialization. I looked rampant, totally animal. My long, dark blonde hair had gone stringy in the humidity; my eyes were wide and hungry. My tits, small and pert at the best of times, rode high on my rib cage, nipples hard and primed. A tide of heat was growing visible on the surface of my skin, from groin to neck. My body was on fire, but what was going on in my mind was way worse. I was almost totally out of control, and yet so in control. That's what this had done to me: this power.

I looked back at Carl and I forgot to be aware of myself, totally. He was struggling with his burden; he was struggling with his need to come. He was so much a victim of my whims. It was that, I realized, that strength contained, that I hungered for. I wanted to feel its potency roar inside me, I wanted to trigger the final release and feel it where it counted most. I threw one leg over his tethered body, straddling his hips, steadying myself with two fingers latched over the rope across his chest. The air rushed between my thighs, over the hot, anxious skin of my hungry pussy.

"That looks so good in your hands," he blurted. He was looking down at my talons, where they bit into the rope. "Oh, yes, that's good." he said, as I flexed my fingers, scratching my nails over his chest. He went to say more, and then his words slipped away and instead, he roared aloud. With one swift gliding action, I had taken him inside.

I was so wet. My inner muscles clasped at his bloated cock. I could feel his balls primed beneath my buttocks when I ground down against his hips. I didn't have long; his face was contorted with ecstasy. I gripped

101

the rope that bound him, and rode him, hard and fast, crushing his cock inside me again and again. The bind of rope along the upper side of his cock added its own pressure and I arched over him, my clit sparking against the surface of the rope, my entire body wired into the multiple stimuli.

"Oh fuck, fuck me," he shouted, rolling his eyes. It was barely perceptible, given his status, but he began to buck his pelvis against his constraints and then his cock lurched and spurted inside me. I grabbed his head in my hands and leaned over, kissing his mouth, crushing my clit on the rope and squeezing his cock hard as he came. Moments later, I threw back my head and roared with my own release.

"You know that hand-made bondage rope you mentioned," I said. Lizzie looked up from her Latte and frowned. Georgina's head snapped round, her eyes bright with interest. She knew me; she knew I wouldn't mouth off. "It really is special isn't it?"

Lizzie grinned. I sipped my cafe negro, whilst winking at Georgina over the rim of the cup.

"Especially when done with true style," I added, smiling, and glanced at my newly manicured fingernails-wine-red, of course, to match Carl's rope. Because it was weeks later and we were still playing. As for my inner sex kitten, I reckon she had become more of a lioness, what with Carl and his rope to toy with, but perhaps I'll let you decide on that score.

THE UPPER HAND

Thwack. Lucinda inhaled sharply and counted to ten while she resisted the urge to stand bolt upright. Heat flared through her flesh where the missile had hit her left buttock. She bit her lip and continued to tend her flowerbeds.

"Bloody kids, you'll be sorry," she muttered to herself.

Her neighbor probably had her sister's children over. There'd been laughter and shuffling from over Diana's fence earlier and the missile, whatever the hell it was, had definitely come from that direction. She moved along the flowerbed with her buttock on fire, and then eased upright as gracefully as she could. She wasn't about to let them know they'd hit home, oh no. With kids you couldn't let them get the better of you. Besides, hopping from foot to foot would provide them with no end of amusement.

She collected her gardening basket, pulled her halter bikini top straight, and headed indoors. Once inside, she gave her buttock a quick rub and ran upstairs to the back bedroom, where she had a good view of next door's garden and could spot the little blighters for later public identification. Easing the Venetian blinds open a crack, she peeped out.

"I'll be damned..." It wasn't kids at all. Instead it was two rather attractive young men that she spied over the fence. One of them was sprawled in a deck chair looking like a reject from a metal band. Wolf-lean, shades on, with baggy shorts and T-shirt complete with offensive slogan, he had straggly hair to his shoulders and a stack of empty beer cans at his side. The other was on his knees, foraging through the undergrowth to spy through a gap in the fence.

"Checking out your target, hmmm," Lucinda murmured, "well, I caught you red handed, you naughty boy."

Because he was bent over in the bushes, she couldn't see too well what he looked like overall, but his rear end was looking pretty good from this angle. Sensing fun, she smiled, her hand going to the exposed part of her buttock, where she'd been hit on a tender spot beneath her high-riding, frayed denim shorts. With a brisk rub of her hand she freed a frisson of sexual pleasure while she took time to observe the view. When the kneeling figure emerged to report to his buddy, a moment later, she let her eyes roam over his naked torso. This one was built and built solid. His hair was shaved close to his head, a zigzag pattern delineating the shape of his skull.

"Very interesting indeed," she murmured when she watched him rubbing his hand over the bulge in his jeans, whilst speaking to his buddy and laughing. They'd obviously been getting off on the view of her rear end while she'd been bent over doing her gardening.

After a good fifteen minutes observation-during which time she came to the realization that Diana's son must be home from University and he'd obviously brought a friend-she began to formulate her plan to take the upper hand with these two lads, because Lucinda wasn't about to let them get away with it, oh no. She hadn't had the pleasure of meeting Diana's son before, but he was about to find out that his target wasn't shy nor easily embarrassed. Star of several explicit art-house movies in the late 'eighties, and currently director of a South London alternative theatre, Lucinda was the type of woman who could envisage the full entertainment potential of a situation like this and had no trouble going after it.

Before she left the upstairs room she hauled her video camera out of the wardrobe and set it up on a tripod, making sure it would catch any activity on the lad's side of the fence, and then she headed back down to the garden, grabbing her sunhat, lotion and shades on the way out.

The August afternoon heat was simmering; the faint hum of insects in the flowerbeds accompanied her own humming as she strode down the garden. She hauled a sun lounger across the lawn and positioned it just about level with the area of their spy hole. Sitting down, she squirmed into her seat deliberately and began rubbing sun lotion into her arms, alert for signs of attention from beyond the fence. By the time she had covered her arms and shoulders in lotion, she picked up a scuffling sound in the bushes beyond the fence. Smiling to herself, she moved to her legs, kicking off her sandals with panache, being sure to apply the lotion in a seductive and suggestive manner. She thought about having the two lads doing this job instead-one on each thigh. Oh yes, she could just picture it, she could almost feel it. Her hand slid up the length of her inner thigh, massaging as it went.

A suppressed comment emitted from the other side of the fence and a muffled conversation followed. She ignored it, because she didn't want contact yet, she was making this an investment for later. The camera upstairs was whirring and so were the visuals in her mind-they'd be clamoring for a view, she'd be willing to bet on it. Would they both be able to see, she wondered, or would they have to fight over one spy hole, like two young bucks infected with midsummer madness.

She set her bottle down and reached for the ties on her halter neck. When she dropped it she heard another sound. She avoided looking directly at the area of their peephole, but a cursory pass-by under cover of her sunglasses definitely showed movement, and a moment later she caught sight of the crown of the shaved head moving at the top of the fence. They were getting sloppy in their eagerness to see what her breasts looked like. That amused her greatly and knowing she had their full attention, she made a big display of squeezing another puddle of lotion into her palm from a height, dribbling it out slowly. Dropping the bottle, she spread the fluid between her hands and then moved to her breasts. Her nipples were already peaked and she sighed loudly as she spread the creamy liquid over the surface of her breasts, massaging it deep.

They'd be aroused and hard now, cocks pounding, had to be.

Her breasts ached with pleasure and an answering thrum in her groin drew her hand lower, across her abdomen and down, into her shorts.

A stifled groan reached her.

They were watching all right. She wasn't about to stop now.

Lucinda decided to watch the video just after sun down, savoring the idea of it while she showered and slipped into a sarong. A large glass of *Chateauneuf-du-Pape* in one hand and the remote in the other, she settled down on the sofa and flicked the video on.

The camera angle was just right, with just a clip of her in one corner as a reference point. She could see her legs from mid-thigh down and she chuckled to herself as she watched the action begin. The shaved head was clued in to her reappearance by the time she was creaming her thighs and gestured for his buddy to join him. The long-haired one clambered out of his deckchair and over to the fence.

They stood still at first, as if disbelief had them in its grip. Then they were jostling for the best view. As time passed their expressions grew serious, tense. Shaved head turned to say something to his buddy as he pulled his cock free of his fly. They whispered and nodded agreement, then began to hunt around. A moment later it seemed as if they located another peephole and they were both stationed close to the fence, eyes trained on the view, cocks out, occasionally turning to each other to pass comment. They were both masturbating vigorously in the bushes, unabashed by each other's presence.

Fascinating, reflected Lucinda, as she toyed with her nipples through the thin sheath of her sarong.

Shaved head was soon gone on it, rubbing at his cock vigorously, face taut with concentration, eyes narrowed as he squinted through the fence. She took a long draft of her wine and sighed. What an absorbing sight that was and how hot it was making her. She slid off the sofa and onto the floor, closer to the screen, legs akimbo on the rug. She flicked her sarong open, her fingers stroking over her tummy and down, remembering how it had been in the garden, when she'd known she'd had an audience. She'd always been a bit of an exhibitionist but this was different: they didn't know she was aware of them watching. This was her voyeuristic journey into their arena, their secret wanking, and their laddish camaraderie over the slut next door.

She'd been brewing for another wank and she fingered her slit, imagining it was their eager young male hands on her, as driven as they were over their cocks right now on the screen. Shaved head was stroking himself fast, concentration honed, and then his head went back as a jet stream of come ribboned into the air and splattered on the fence. The toes of her left foot stroked down the side of the screen while she watched the wolf-lean one trying to watch through the gap in the fence and wank himself off. What a sight it was when he finally came.

"Oh boy," she murmured, and thrust harder, her clit bound in pleasure under the pressure of the palm of her hand, two fingers inside, slick and moving frantically. Her sex was on fire, her hips bucking up from the floor. The whirring of the video and the sounds of her pleasure-fuelled sex filled the silent room. And she had the remote; she could fast forward and rewind just as much as she wanted. Knowing they were so hot for her and being able to watch it over and again was a heady intoxicant and she eked out her pleasure that evening for just as long as she could bare another self-induced orgasm.

Diana enjoyed cut flowers. Lucinda preferred to see them growing in the beds, but for the sake of her project she cut an armful and took them round to her neighbor's house the next day. She'd waited until late afternoon, when the lads had taken up residence in the garden and had already downed a few cans of their favored brew.

"They're beautiful, thank you dear," Diana said as she took the bouquet and ushered Lucinda after her while she put them in water.

In the oak and marble kitchen Lucinda gravitated towards the window that overlooked the garden. "It's another glorious day," she commented. Out in the garden the two lads were stretching like waking tomcats, reclaiming their territory, sprawling in the summer warmth. "Oh, is that your son home from Uni?"

"Yes that's Jamie. And the one with the hair," she rolled her eyes, "he calls himself Man, although I don't think that's his real name."

"Man, ay." Lucinda smiled as she watched Jamie cavorting in the sun. He was definitely the showman. And Man was the quieter, long-haired, wolf-like one. She was determined to find out what they would be like in closer proximity.

She turned back to her neighbor. "It must be great having two strapping lads around, to help you out with chores and such."

Diana gave a derisive laugh. "Well, I daresay they'd help out in an emergency but they aren't ones to put themselves forward for any task that doesn't instantly appeal to them." She smiled over the flowers, now stashed in a vase. "The garden and the beer seem to have held their attention pretty solidly these past few days. I was out yesterday and when I got home Man had somehow picked up a rash from the bushes and both of them were in danger of getting burnt from over exposure."

Lucinda enjoyed her secret thoughts for a moment. "Are they going to be around for long?"

"Until next week, then they're off to some rock festival in Wales."

"Hmm, in that case would you mind if I borrowed them for an hour or two? I've got one of those self-assembly shelf units that I need a hand with."

"Feel free, I'm sure the offer of a beer or two might sway them."

"I'm sure you're right." Lucinda replied and smiled. "I'll take your advice and offer plenty of tempting bait."

And she knew just what sort of bait they liked best.

Up close they were just as attractive, if not more so. "Hello, Boys," she said, trying to suppress her grin as she noticed Jamie's eyebrows shoot up at the sight of her on this side of the fence. Man shielded his eyes against the sun for a better look. "If it's not too much trouble, I'd like to drag you away from your afternoon sun-worship."

"This is Lucinda, our neighbor," Diana explained. "She needs a hand with some bookshelves; can you two make yourself useful and help her out?"

"I'll make it worth your while," Lucinda interjected.

The two men glanced at each other for support. After a moment they got to their feet.

Once she'd led them round to her place and got them inside, she pointed out the Ikea flat pack in the sitting room and told them she'd get them some beers. Like two hungry hounds that had been thrown a scrap from a plate but sensed the real juicy meat was being kept somewhere nearby, they worked with the chore they'd been given while looking forlornly in her direction.

The floor was soon covered in packaging, but when she got back their eyes were trained on her. Not surprisingly, she was as provocatively dressed as yesterday, if not more so. She had a great figure for a woman knocking forty years and she knew how to show it off to its best advantage. And she was enjoying every moment of their lascivious eyes on her.

"It's so hard for a single woman to manage a big erection," she said, idly, as she handed them their drinks. Jamie nearly dropped his can; Man swore under his breath and two patches of color appeared on his gaunt cheekbones.

Nice to see we're all on the same wavelength, even if they don't know it yet.

"I really appreciate you helping me out."

"Any time, Lucinda," Jamie offered, grinning widely, glancing over at his friend and winking conspiratorially.

That was enough of that, she was in control here. She walked over to the sofa and lifted the remote. "Carry on," she said. "I want to see what you make of it." She flicked the video player on.

Dutifully, they turned back to the job they had been assigned to. Lucinda smiled, they were pleasantly malleable and that suited her well. She fast forwarded through a rather fine BBC production of The Merchant of Venice until she felt it was time, and then casually swapped over the videos.

The two of them floundered to a standstill when they caught sight of themselves on the TV screen.

"You were watching us," Jamie murmured.

"I was, but then you were watching me. Fair exchange is no robbery." Her eyes flicked back and forth from them to the TV. "Quite a sight, isn't it?" she added, raising her glass to them.

"Oh shit," Man declared, flushing when he saw himself wanking on screen.

"Oh, please, don't be coy. You've got nothing to be ashamed of."

Jamie was a little more in touch with what might be on offer, weighing up what he saw on the screen and what she was showing him: a knowing smile, an enticing glance, a hand nonchalantly linked over the belt of her low-slung shorts, fingers tapping over the zipper.

He set down the assembly instructions he had in his hand. "You knew all along. You went along with it, and filmed it?"

She nodded.

"So why have you brought us round here, really?"

She purred. "Oh, I liked what I saw and I think you owe me a closer look, in the flesh, as it were." She couldn't keep the dirty smile off her face. "You wouldn't object to giving me a repeat performance, up close, would you?"

Jamie grinned. "I'm up for it." He put his hand on the bulge in his jeans. He really did love that cock of his! He turned to his friend. "Manfred?"

111

Man flicked him a disapproving glance at the use of his full name, but nodded. His lean, hungry looks matched the expression in his eyes.

A bolt of sexual power hit her, pure and undiluted. She moved, kneeling up on the sofa. "Right then, I'm sure you won't mind me having a more active role, this time around?"

They both shook their heads. Man had a wild look in his eyes.

This is so good. The power rush alone was getting her wet. And they were both sloping closer, hounds with their eyes on the main dish. She had a split second to decide, but she was a very naughty girl at heart and she couldn't resist. She reached into her pocket and pulled out the condom she had stashed there. Flipping it towards the strewn packaging and abandoned shelves she said: "whoever finds that gets to fuck me; the other has to give me a show."

They stared at her, open-mouthed, for a whole five seconds and then reacted; the pair of them scrabbling amongst the cardboard and bubble wrap to find the packet. Lucinda couldn't help chuckling, wishing she had her camera.

Man jumped up triumphantly with the prize in his hands.

Perfect.

"Oh, bloody hell," Jamie muttered. "That's not fair."

"It is fair, besides, you have no right to complain about anything, since you smacked me on the arse yesterday!"

He pouted.

She pulled her top off, squeezing her breasts in her hands right at him. "Stay where you are. Man, come round here, I want you to fuck me from behind, while

Jamie watches." She wriggled her shorts down her thighs, leaning over the back of the sofa.

Jamie's eyes were black with lust. He had his zipper open. He grunted his disapproval when Man took up his position behind her, but started wanking almost immediately. What a sight! A dribble of moisture followed her shorts down her thighs.

"Oh, yes," she moaned. Man had dipped his fingers tentatively into her slit and was stroking his way back and forth from clit into her wet hole. "Keep going, you're right on target!" He did as requested for a few moments before he cursed under his breath and she heard the sound the condom being ripped open. She pushed her bottom back, inviting him in, her eyes on the incredible tightness of the muscles on Jamie's arms and torso while he rode his cock with his fist, his hips arched up, his mouth tight as he watched.

Man plowed into her, his cock filling her, then rolling in and out, bashing her breasts against back of the sofa with his urgency. Moments later his fingers groped and hit her clit; she arched again, and his balls hit home. She contracted on him, her body on fire. She groaned and pressed her nipples hard on the sofa, moaning loudly as she hit the jackpot.

"Come closer," she urged Jamie, as she surfaced. He shuffled forward. She stuck her tongue out, and licked the drop of come from the end of his prick. She was starting to come again. He moaned, his eyes frantic. "Come on my tits, baby," she said. He did, a split second later, just as Man exploded inside her.

"You are one hot lady," Man said when he collapsed on the sofa beside her.

"Yeah," Jamie agreed. "I hope you have plenty more bookshelves for us to erect," he added, with more than a hint of suggestive sarcasm.

"Loads," she confirmed, winking at him approvingly. "But next time I really must film you getting it up."

"You drive a hard bargain, but it's a deal," he replied, and Man nodded, laughing.

Not bad for a day's work, Lucinda reflected, and made a note to buy more video tape for her new personal video collection: the upper hand in action.

COUNTING THE DAYS

Thank God it's Friday. I'd been counting the days off, and boy, had they ever dragged. But I figured that if I could get to the end of the first week, I could maybe make it to week two.

Maybe.

I just had to prove I could make it through my one-month contract. Biting the bullet and taking an office job had been the absolute pits in the first place, but I couldn't drift from college course to college course any longer. The time had come to quell my rebellious streak, tame my multicolored mop of hair, take out my nose ring and don an acceptably smart outfit. What a crime, I thought to myself, when I'd packed away my usual, much more alternative wardrobe, and headed for the temp agency.

The job I was assigned to was deadly. I was audio typing debt-collecting letters for a junior lawyer, and William had been junior forever. He stumbled into my office, blushing to the roots of his remaining few hairs, and deposited a stack of files and tapes on my desk. That was day one. Since day two, he'd left the stacks on my desk before I even got in, presumably in order not to have to make small talk with me, and then disappeared off to who knew where. Maybe he was expecting a simpering office mouse, not a frustrated rebel who responded sarcastically when he mentioned the pleasant weather we were having for the time of year.

Well, what did he expect?

The weather was outside the tinted windows and I was trapped inside. There was no decent company to chat with on breaks and there wasn't even any eye candy in the vicinity. The building site opposite my nineteenth-story window was too far away to make out anything. That would have been something. All I got was a drifting tide of muck curtaining my window courtesy of the builder's activities, no brawny guys to check out. Perhaps if I brought in a pair of binoculars I could get a better look, and if I got a better look, that might break up the monotony.

Mostly there was just me and Audrey in the offices. Audrey was the senior administrator and she sat reading magazines and filing her nails all day in the reception. She looked down her nose at me condescendingly whenever I came out of my cell for a coffee. The highlight of her work schedule seemed to be shuffling wannabe-divorcees into the senior partner's office, giving appropriate murmurs of concern to their irate monologues about truant husbands. I wouldn't have been able to keep a straight face. Perhaps that's why I wasn't on the front desk.

Looking at the clock, I stood up. It was nearly midday, time for my third caffeine shot of the day. Thank God it was Friday. I was about to step out from behind my desk when darkness suddenly descended. I froze. A shadow had fallen across me from behind, from the window situated behind my desk. The shadow moved across the surface of the desk. My heart beat faster as I tried to make sense of it. Nothing had broken the light falling in the window all week. What could it be?

I turned and took in the sight that met my eyes. Standing in a suspended safety cradle was a window cleaner, moving a large squeegee over the surface of the glass with a rhythmic agility, all the while watching me and grinning cheekily. He winked, obviously well aware he'd given me a fright. I managed to return his smile and waved at him, snatching up my cup from the desk to cover my awkwardness.

Something interesting had finally happened! And, yes, he was interesting. Ruggedly good looking, with several days' worth of stubble, tall, well-built and bleached blonde. He went about his work in a showy, nonchalant way that made it look like a warm-up for dirty dancing. He moved his entire body, as if dancing to the music he was listening to via his headset, and rode his massive squeegee easily over the surface of the glass, his biceps flexing, his torso riding firm and strong beneath the t-shirt he was wearing. Sexy! My blood pumped quicker when I noticed he was eyeing me speculatively, from head to toe. I leaned one hip up against the desk, toying with the mug in my hands, taking in the sight. Well, why not? He was doing the same.

When he'd finished his task he dropped the squeegee, reached into his pocket and pulled something out. It was a piece of paper. He scribbled on it with a stub of pencil, then held it up against the glass for me to read. I stepped closer and read the scrawled message.

Great Legs. Next time wear a shorter skirt.

I smiled, I couldn't help it. He grinned, saluted and hit a control panel, hanging easily on the ropes as the safety cradle disappeared from view.

Well, that had woken me up. Wear a shorter skirt? What a card! Sure, I was up for some fun and games, especially with a hunk like him, but when was the "next time" that he was referring to? There was only one way to find out.

"I just had the most amazing shock," I said to Audrey, as I poured filter coffee into my mug. "Some guy was hanging on the outside of the building cleaning the windows."

Audrey gave me a superior smile. "Not what you expect to see this high up, is it?"

"Not exactly. How often do they come around? I'd like to be prepared next time?"

"Oh, usually every six weeks."

My heart sank. I'd be finished with my contract and gone by the next time he appeared.

"Until they started the building work opposite," she added. "It's every Friday on that side of the building now, so you'll have to be prepared for another visit next week."

"Oh, I will be," I said, as I sidled off, trying to contain my smile.

That second week went much quicker. In fact, counting the days off till Friday took on a whole new meaning. I was looking forward to my visitor, instead of wishing the days away until the end of my contract. I didn't even think of bringing the binoculars in; I had something far more interesting to focus on: the arrival of the dishy window cleaner. What would happen if I did as he suggested and wore a shorter skirt? Where would it go then? I raced through my stacks of audio typing whilst at the back of my mind I tried to decide what to wear.

Audrey commented on the fact that my typing had speeded up. She had so little to do; she had to eavesdrop on me to fill her timetable. If it weren't for the prospect of the window guy, I would have told her to stick her job. She didn't approve of me, that much was obvious from the start. I'd heard her on the phone to the temp agency, asking if they had "anyone more suitable, someone the right caliber to work in a legal office." Too bad for her they didn't have anyone else, right? And she did so not approve when I arrived for work on that second Friday, wearing the leather mini skirt I usually saved for clubbing, knee length boots and a skin-tight lizard print shirt that dipped low into my cleavage. I waved when I passed her desk where she sat open-mouthed, glaring at my outfit.

The morning went far too slowly and I was up and pacing around between the desk and the window when the shadow of the cradle finally began to descend. This time I was even more mesmerized, because as the window cleaner lowered into my field of vision I realized he was stripped to the waist. Boy, what a sight for sore eyes that was. He was built all right, all that physical labor had given him a great body and the day was warm enough for him to sun himself while he worked. He grinned, eyeing me appreciatively as he washed the window. I reached for a piece of paper and wrote him a message.

Great abs! Do you approve of the skirt length?

When he broke into a laugh, I'd have paid highly to hear the sound of it. He nodded, his mouth forming a whistle while he eyed the gap between my boots and the skirt. With his eyes on me like that, I was suddenly aware of every inch of my body. My breasts felt tight. My sex was heavy, responsive to every signal he was giving me, to every nuance of his body language. I turned on my heel and gave him a better look, hands on hips. He reached into his pocket and scribbled on his notepad, slamming the paper against the glass.

Oh yeah. That's much better, but I still can't see what color your underwear is.

I laughed. What a lad. And something about the set up, with him on the other side of the glass like that, made me feel even more daring than I might have under normal circumstances, and I was no shrinking violet either way.

His squeegee was hanging idly in one hand, the other leaned up against the taut ropes of the safety cradle as he watched, riveted while I slid one finger down into the

119

front of my shirt, idly toying with the top button in my cleavage. He licked his lips. My sex clenched; my panties were already damp from expectation. Seeing him through the barrier of the impermeable glass had created a void of discovery, a safe zone to test each other out. I popped my top button, thrilled by the effect I was having on him. He mouthed something encouraging. I let another button pop open. He nodded, one hand gesturing for me to continue. I felt like I was part of an act in a live sex show. The thought spurred me on. I stepped closer to the glass. We were possibly twelve inches apart, but he was so untouchable. I undid the final two buttons, my hands pushing the fabric back to reveal my sheer lace bra.

He shook his head; his eyes glazed, and he ran one finger down the length of the glass in front of my breasts, smearing the damp glass with his touch. He continued to stare while he grappled in his pocket for his paper and pencil and wrote me another note:

You've made my day! Will I get to see more of you next week?

He scrunched the paper in his hand after I read it, and his eyes were molten with arousal. I nodded, and blew him a kiss, winking. As he reached for the controls on his cradle, his other hand ran over the impressive bulge in his jeans, and he flickered his eyebrows at me. Then he was gone. Only the smear on the glass remained to remind me of what had passed between us, a sticky remark on the intervening sheer pane. I touched the inside of the glass, placing my own mark against his. Man, was he ever sexy. And he was making me so hot. I stalked over to the air conditioning panel and turned it up to full blast, my mind racing with ideas of how to up the ante the following week.

By the time that third Friday came around, I'd been thinking on it long and hard-I'd even dreamt about the guy twice. Both times it was the live sex show imagery, and the idea of it fascinated me. In the first dream, I was dancing for him, slow and sexy. He was riveted, sitting back in a low chair, his erection straining through his jeans. In the second dream, I stripped naked and then watched as he tried to lick my body through the glass. When I woke, I was twisted in my sheets, my fingers crushed between my legs as I wanked myself off.

My excitement level built over the week and my imagination was running riot. To top it all, Audrey had pissed me off big time, which left me feeling even more rebellious. I was ready to pull pints in my local pub rather than listen to her miserable condescension a moment longer. That sense of rebellion and the fact the guy had filled my thoughts all week long meant that I was edgy and high on my own physical arousal.

"Thank God it's Friday," I murmured to myself, yet again. But this time I smiled at the idea.

The window cleaner looked at my floating summer dress with a surprised expression when he winched down into view. I waved and then turned my chair to face the window, to face him. I sat down in it, staring straight at him, smiling. He wrote his message:

> *Hey, you're breaking my heart here. That skirt is way too long.*

He mimed an aching heart, his expression teasing me all the while. I shook my head at him, swinging my chair from side to side, then I kicked back in the chair, one strappy, sandaled foot jamming up against the window frame, the dress sliding down my thighs and pooling in my groin.

Oh yeah, he loved that.

121

I pivoted on one heel, my chair moving from side to side. I knew he was watching the flash of scarlet G-string I was wearing and it fuelled my fire. Between my thighs, a nagging pulse begged for attention. I let my hand tease along the hemline of the dress. He lifted his head, his eyes on my fingers. I picked up the piece of paper I'd left handy and scribbled on it:

What do you think now?

Quickly, he replied.

I'd like to put my hands under it and touch you.

It was just the kind of response that I'd hoped for. He was really up for this. I ran my hand over the surface of my G-string, one finger sliding beneath the fabric. He nodded his head, scribbling again.

You are so bad!

"You better believe it," I whispered, as I pushed my fingers into my damp slit, where my clit was begging for attention. With a quick, practiced action, I arrested it between two fingers, my whole body jolting with the sensations that instantaneously roared over me.

The guy started craning his neck, like he could see inside my underwear if he tried hard enough. Logic had clearly gone from his mind by that point. For me, the fact that one gorgeous man was watching, wanting me, completely mesmerized by what I was doing, was like a drug heightening the experience, channeling every dart of pleasure into a major roller-coaster ride. I slid down in the chair, my back arching against it as I worked my clit. My fingers were sticky, the flimsy fabric of my G-string quickly growing wet. His mouth was moving-he was saying something to himself and his eyes were glazed with lust.

"Yes," I whispered at his silent form, "yes." I managed to nod at him, my lips parting, when my clit throbbed unbearably and density gathered in my core. As I rode the wave, I became aware that he was moving. The cradle was disappearing out of view. Had I gone too far? Had I embarrassed the poor guy? I doubted it-he'd pushed it along this far. And I'd really got off on the secret, silent performance for the man on the other side of the glass. My body was thrumming with sensation, my energy levels soaring.

I let my foot slide down from the window. I couldn't help thinking about how it might have looked to him, from the outside. Perhaps he'd gone off somewhere more discreet to have a wank. The idea infused me with a sense of raw power, heady and intoxicating. That was when I heard voices outside.

"Fuck." I tried to pull myself together.

There was some sort of disagreement going on in the corridor. Audrey sounded put out. I grappled my dress into place, spinning my chair to face front. The door sprang open.

"There must be some mistake," Audrey said, in a bewildered tone. "We had them done just a few weeks ago."

"It's contracted, trust me."

I blinked, several times. It was him. He was there, standing in the doorway to my office. He'd put his t-shirt on, come inside and found my office-and now he was walking in. Dumping a bucket on the floor, he grinned at me and slammed the door shut behind him. A stifled cry of dismay emitted from beyond the door.

Now what was I going to do? No glass shield, no gap the equivalent of thousands of square feet separating us. My blood roared, my heart thumping out a fierce,

123

erratic rhythm. Given that I was already totally wired by what had gone before, his one-hundred-percent physical presence tripped switches I didn't even know I had.

"Sorry to interrupt, but I couldn't resist." He put his hands on his hips, observing me with hungry, watchful eyes. He was even sexier in the flesh, and the sound of his voice ran torrents of sensation over me. I was delirious with arousal, unable to stop myself responding in kind.

"Couldn't resist seeing it in the flesh, huh?"

He strode over. Pure testosterone oozed from him. Had I really caused this? Tut-tut, I mused-must be more circumspect around rampant males. I had to laugh. I couldn't believe he'd actually fought his way past Audrey and was standing right there inside the office.

"You better believe it. That performance was enough to drive a man insane." He knelt down and swung my chair round so it faced him. His eyes were green, bright green. I ran a finger over his stubbed chin. He captured it in one strong hand, giving me a look that announced he was taking control of the situation now.

"I had to get me a closer look." The smile he gave me was full of raw, undiluted sex appeal.

Before I knew what was happening, he'd grabbed my legs and hauled them apart. If I thought my little bout of exhibitionist self-pleasuring had been hot, I wasn't prepared for what came next.

He ran his hands down the inside of my thighs, feeling his way toward the hot niche at their juncture. He stripped my soaked g-string down my legs, manhandling me with ease. The way he looked at me where I was wet from pleasure, sent a hot wave of self-awareness over me. Then I suddenly forgot how to be self-aware when the tip of his tongue found its way into the sticky, cloying heat of my slit and he was eating me up. I nearly lifted off the chair!

His tongue was agile and intuitive. He explored the territory of my sex, before he began mouthing me, his tongue lapping against my swollen lips and over the jutting flesh of my clit. Rivers of sensation flew through my groin. My hands were knotting in his hair, my hips bucking against him. When he pushed an inquisitive finger inside me I quickly came a second time, my body shuddering.

"Do you do this with every woman you meet courtesy of your squeegee?" I managed to ask, as I surfaced.

"Nope, most of them do a runner when I appear. Not you though." He gave me that suggestive smile of his. He had one hand resting on his crotch, where he was rock hard inside his jeans. I was just contemplating how quickly I would hit the jackpot a third time if I had the pleasure of something that hard inside me, when I heard a sound.

"You're fired." It was Audrey. She stood in the doorway, her hands gripping the frame, glowering.

"Too late, I quit." Let's face it; it was only a matter of time before I walked out or got fired. It had been well worth it.

"I'm sorry," the guy whispered, one hand squeezing my thigh rather endearingly. He was genuinely concerned. What a sweetie.

"No problem, really. I was out of here anyway." I leaned forward and pushed my fingers into his hair, hauling his head back. I kissed his mouth deep and hard, reveling in the sense of deviance that roared in my veins.

I glanced over just as Audrey staggered backwards in the doorway, shocked to the core by my response, her mouth opening and closing like a fish's.

The man kneeling between my legs followed my gaze and chuckled low. "If you're looking for a new job, we need a receptionist at HQ. It's not a posh place like this, but we have a laugh, and it does mean I'd get to see you again."

125

His smile sent an aftershock of pleasure right through me.

"Not to mention the fact that a chick like you would be a hell of a lot more fun than the dragon they sent us from the agency."

"You reckon?" I asked, pushing him onto the floor on his back, straddling him and reaching for his belt.

"I reckon," he said, grinning widely when he felt my hand reach for his cock.

What was the old saying about being in the right place at the right time, and grabbing opportunities when they come by? My hand tightened on his cock. It looked like office work wasn't going to be so bad after all.

THE INNER VIXEN

Daniel is kneeling before me. I walk around him, my paces measured, my long leather boots making a quiet but insistent sound as they brush together. They're all I'm wearing. Daniel is stripped to the waist, his arms cuffed behind him. I'm admiring his body, so leanly muscular as he kneels on the floor before me, resting on his haunches, his torso upright and proud. As I consider the fact that he is mine, my willing pet, power plumes through me. As if it were a heady sexual elixir, I thrive on it. My core tightens and my sex grows damper with each passing moment.

His head moves imperceptibly as he watches me, and I revel in his adoring gaze. His cock is hard inside his faded black jeans, but I know he likes that confinement, just as he likes his wrists bound behind his back while I survey him. He's so alert, so taut with restrained desire. I feel it pouring out of him and it empowers me more.

As I walk on, circling him, I reach over, pull a chair close behind him and sit. Over his shoulder, I see our reflection in the mirror. He's looking too, and it's the perfect image of woman and lover.

I trace one hand down his back. His muscles ripple and I know he's longing for more, for a more vivid assault on his senses: the whip. Making him wait, I sit back in the chair, lift my foot and rest one stiletto heel between his shoulder blades, edging him forward. He pivots against it and groans aloud, his body arched. I know just how much pain he wants, how much he needs. My body responds to his reaction, heat rising to the surface of my skin. My inner vixen is revving up to full throttle, the essential me-the inner woman that Daniel recognized and introduced me to.

"How did you know that I would respond?" I asked him the night we met.

"I saw her, your inner vixen. I wanted to know her. I wanted to experience her."

So did I.

That's how it began.

We met at an alternative music event. I was there to photograph it for a guide promoting local gigs. I went alone, which I usually did when I was working. I dressed strong, which meant people wouldn't bother me-Doc Martens, black combat pants with a studded belt, cropped sports bra, bare midriff, my tribal tattoos on display.

It was a hot night and the heat was rising from the pavements. Inside the pub venue I found the performance room was a large space upstairs, filling fast with the alternative crowd, black wearing fetishists and goths. I stationed myself by a pillar near the front, where I had a good view of both stage and audience. The atmosphere was already humming with energy when the music kicked off.

I was busy photographing the first band when I became aware of someone watching me. I scanned the crowd. The man caught my eye and, as he did, he acknowledged me, quickly smiling and walking over. All in black, he was a studious type with shaggy hair and a lean whip strong countenance.

He ducked in against my head to speak over the music, introducing himself, commenting on what I was up to. "Nice camera, is this a hobby?"

"Started that way. It's work, this time around. I'm photographing the gig for a new music magazine."

He nodded. "I haven't seen you in the scene before."

"I just moved from the other side of London." I nodded my head to the people behind him. "Looks like a fun crowd."

"You better believe it." His smile held so much mischief I was immediately affected by it.

Looking back at how events unfolded that night I often contemplate how surprised I would have been if I had known where it was going. I tried not to get too distracted from the job as I answered his questions. There was something compelling about him but I couldn't put my finger on it. Was it because he was looking so attentively at me?

During the gap between the bands I took a break to chat properly. He started to talk about astronomy, of all things. Intelligent and amusing, I was quickly laughing, unable to stop enjoying the rapid-fire conversation he initiated. The crowd moved around us, a parade of peacocks, a blur of black, velvet, shiny, metal-studded -a feast for the senses. The DJ music between the bands had my pulse racing, or was it because of Daniel's attention and the fact it was all mine? All mine. Like a devotee. Oh, yes, I was hooked, even though I didn't yet know why.

When he made the move, he did it subtly, never breaking his conversation. He reached inside his biker jacket and pulled out a small, soft leather object. He turned it in his hands, attracting my attention to it. I saw that it was a leather head mask. He looked up suddenly, and stopped talking.

He was measuring my reaction to the object he held.

My pulse tripped and then raced on, fascination flickering inside me.

His eyes narrowed, glinting, his smile so wickedly mischievous and attractive. I couldn't stop myself returning it. Behind him I saw that people were looking our way. Part of me wanted to walk away. Whatever game he was playing with me right there at the front of the venue was going to attract attention. But he triggered something inside me, and it was because of his demeanor,

129

somehow respectful, and intrinsically sexy. It tugged at my curiosity, and aroused me.

"Will you lace me in?" He paused, his eyes scrutinizing as I considered the remark.

Something was unfolding inside me, and it was something big, overwhelming.

I nodded, still smiling. I'd never done anything like this before, but the adventure had me firmly in its grasp. He pulled the mask over his head. It moved easily into place pushing his hair down and outlining his head, starkly. The leather was polished black, reflecting the stage lights as he turned and dipped down to let me tie the laces that ran down the back of his skull to the nape of the neck.

Oh, how that simple act affected me, fuelling me for what was to come.

My camera dangled from my neck as I moved into place. The laces felt good in my hands, and I enjoyed the feeling of control I got when I pulled the soft leather into place. It hugged tight against his skull, enclosing him. Even though I tried to concentrate on the task, I was acutely aware of my own reaction to it, and the attention we were generating from the crowd beyond. People were watching, and somehow that made it all the more arousing.

When I was done, he turned back to me, his eyes twinkling through the peepholes. Incredibly, he unzipped the mouth and continued his conversation as before. The second band came onstage. The singer, a striking punk in leather jeans and a studded corset, strutted the stage as she sang, twin keyboard players behind her moving to the drum and bass sound. Daniel and I shifted to the music at first and then, without warning, he dropped to his knees before me. Resting back on his haunches he looked up at me adoringly. Laughter escaped me and his eyes twinkled as I reached out and put my hand on his head, instinctively. I could almost feel him urging me on. Something certainly was, and I was getting high on the rush it delivered. After I stroked his head, he rubbed it against my thighs in an affectionate catlike way, first one side, than the other. It was an incredibly sensual thing to do and my pussy was getting hotter and damper all the time. Arousal and self-awareness of the observers affected me strangely. I couldn't quite believe it, and for some reason I couldn't stop smiling. It was different from how I might have thought, because it felt so right. Something inside of me was responding to him, and it felt good.

"You're diverting attention from the band," I teased, when he stood up, speaking close against his head so he could hear me.

"Ah, but they don't mind, they are friends." He looked toward the stage and as he did I realized the singer had been watching him and she was beaming. She winked at me. I felt welcomed, part of it, and oddly at home.

Daniel reached inside his leather jacket again, his hand resting there. What would it be this time, I wondered with anticipation. From the pocket, he pulled out a whip, a cat-o'-nine-tails with its leather strands wound tight around the handle. A whip. I watched as he ran the strands through his fingers, untangling them. My heart was pounding. I couldn't imagine where the situation was going next. Just thinking about it set me on a roller coaster of emotions. Over his shoulder, I saw that several members of the audience were completely riveted. Men. Hungry men, with envy in their eyes. Did they think we were together? That we were part of the show?

Before I had time to wonder any more, the singer jumped from the stage and strode toward us as she belted out the lyrics of her song. She took the whip from Daniel and pointed it at the floor. I watched, riveted as he knelt and curled over. Moving to the music, she thrashed his upper body through his leather jacket. As he pulled the jacket tight I became aware that there was something under it. Daniel was wearing a bondage harness under his clothes. My pussy clenched.

The singer handed me the whip and smiled, before leaping back onto the stage. She hovered at our side of the stage, where the light poured down on to us. There was a moment of fear, a moment of confusion, and then it happened: a rampant urge to do it, to take control, rose up inside me, as if a switch had been tripped. I knew what to do, and why. I stepped over to where he was crouching, looking up at me with expectation. I clenched the handle of the whip, running the strands of leather across my other hand. What would it feel like, whipping a man? My body told me how it would feel: good. Any doubt I had was pushed aside as I reminded myself that he wanted it, and he enjoyed this. So would I.

The audience had created a semicircle around him, and I stepped in front of them facing toward the stage. Music pounded in my ears, powering me up even more. My senses were being overloaded, and yet I was strangely honed and clear-headed. I was in this scene. More than that, I was in control of it now.

Oh god, how good it felt. I was wet, my sex clenching.

I ran the strands of leather across his back, testing it out. The line of his bondage harness was obvious now. As I considered how it might feel for him, and for me, something flared inside me: need, and desire. I thrashed him across the back of one shoulder, then the other, moving in rhythmic patterns. He flinched at each thrash and my pussy gushed. The rush of power I got, heady and deviant, startled me with its intensity. Pleasure ripped through me. I bent down and put my hand under his jacket and T-shirt, grasping for the harness. Pushing my fingers under it, I gripped, applying enough tension so that he would feel it all over his body.

His hands went to the floor, bracing himself, and I knew I had tuned into something. "You naughty boy," I said with delight, against his head.

Shame poured out of him.

I lifted and stepped away from him, returning to my pillar at the stage, the whip dangling from my hand. My heart was pounding. I couldn't believe what I'd just done and most of all I couldn't believe the way it made me feel. Daniel rose to his hands and knees and followed me over, like a pet panther. He stayed by my feet for the rest of the gig, his head rubbing against me affectionately. As I stroked his head in between taking photographs of the band onstage, a feeling of inner calm washed over me. Even though I was still aroused, startled and confused by my reaction, it was like a feeling of honesty and true realization.

This has empowered me.

The whole experience had been like sex itself, with its arousal, its peak and its transcendence. I'd had no clue I would enjoy dominating a man, whipping him publicly, but I had. And judging from the adoration at my feet, it was a two-way street.

As the gig ended the lights went up and everyone was suddenly far too real for me. I didn't want the staring eyes anymore. I needed a drink. I needed space to think through what had happened to me. The band members were with Daniel; he was on his feet and chatting. Maybe if it hadn't have been me, he would have gone to someone else. Whatever his reason for choosing me to approach, it had altered my life. Grabbing my stuff, I headed to the bar downstairs, where I ordered a double shot and downed it quickly. My legs were like jelly as I put down the glass and made ready to leave. Daniel was on his way down the stairs, and the mask was gone.

I wanted to go home and think about it, savor the strange sense of euphoria that had overcome me back there. But if I left now, would I ever see him again? Unsure how far I wanted to go along this path, I headed for the door and out into the street. It had rained and the street was different from when I had gone inside. So was I. I ran up the hill, passing underneath the railway arches toward the station. When I heard his footsteps echoing under the arches behind me, I knew it was him. I stopped and turned back to look at him.

He held up his hands in a sign of peace. "I wasn't going to come after you, but something made me."

I nodded. I wasn't afraid of him; I realized it was me that I was afraid of. The unknown me who had risen up so quickly, so unexpectedly. My inner vixen, as I would later identify her.

"You were so good," he whispered and reached to stroke my arm affectionately.

"Why did you come over to me?"

"I could tell you wanted to play. You did, didn't you?"

He was right, but he had known and I hadn't. That was unnerving. He was still stroking my arms. I noticed that we felt like equals now, in fact his seductive movement against my skin felt like he was taking charge of me now. Uncertainty reigned. "I have to go."

"Don't go. Don't deny it." He smiled hopefully but I saw a flicker of regret in his eyes. He thought I was leaving.

"I've never done this before," I confessed, needing him to know that.

He stared at me, and then after a moment he stepped closer, that mischievous smile of his surfacing. With his hands around my upper arms I felt strangely secure, and yet curious and aching for more. A complete stranger had this effect on me? It was because he recognized his opposite, in me. The thought crossed my mind, and I didn't reject it.

134

"Did you want to do it again? Did you want to do more? Somewhere private, perhaps?"

Images flashed through my mind, images brought on by that suggestion, images of fantasies I hadn't ever recognized that I had, but were suddenly growing fast and multiplying in my mind, assailing me with their erotic potential, their absolute promise of pleasure.

"Maybe," I murmured.

We stood there in the gloom of the damp tunnel, with the sound of cars driving through the rainy streets surrounding us. There was no need to say more. When his head dipped and his lips brushed over mine, my inner vixen whispered to me: don't turn away.

I didn't.

I couldn't.

And so here we are, months later and I am so glad I didn't turn away that night. Reaching down, I unbind him before I grab the whip. The mark of my heel on his back is like the center of a bull's eye. I use it to focus me because whipping him gives me such a rush I need that anchor. When I'm done and he is shuddering with need, I step in front of him.

His forehead rests against my pussy. "Thank you, mistress."

I feel his breath on my skin, the brush of his forehead across my naked mons. I want him to fill me, physically, as he has filled me emotionally and spiritually. "Lie down," I instruct.

He rolls onto his back, opening his fly, knowing what I want, never once breaking eye contact with me. His cock bounces free, long and hard, oozing. Climbing over him, I lift and lower, taking him inside, my sex hungrily eating him up while my boots bite into his flanks. Looking down at him, I know that what Daniel saw in me may never have been revealed by anyone else, and that makes me snatch at him, my nails driving into his shoulders as I grind down onto his cock. He recognized her in me before I did. He told me he could see her, showing me the real me.

I make love to him fast and hard. Taking him, using him, devouring everything he gives, until his body bucks up under me. He spurts inside me and then I come, with loud and determined force, reveling in the sense of power and release. The inner vixen, risen and reigning supreme.

LIVE TONIGHT

Naomi was aroused, because live music always gave her a sexual thrill. For Naomi, no other way of experiencing music came close to this, and this was like good sex for her, the best kind-hot and horny and unbridled, the kind where you can't wait to debauch yourself and get off. Something about the atmosphere and the way the music surrounded her, pounding up through the floor, really got to her. It flooded her senses and gave her a totally unique kind of high. Naomi often felt as if she were an extra instrument, as if her body was being played along with the instruments on the stage-and that sense of being played was what did it for her.

It had to be a public performance. She couldn't re-create it at home. The club scene was good, but not unique enough. She also liked smaller venues and pub bands but could never lose herself in the environment quite as well as she could at a large venue, and that was the key. Only there did the experience become so intense that her pulse pounded and her underwear got hot and damp within moments. By the end of the concert she'd have to go to the ladies' toilets to wank, before she made her way home. With her back up against one wall of the cubicle and her foot wedged on the opposite wall, she'd shove her hand inside her underwear and rub herself hard, forcing out all that built up arousal. She had to take that last step, otherwise she was a wreck by the time she got home, as if she'd been taken to the very edge of orgasm and left there, wired and yet incomplete. She was always close, fast at her peak, the complete high of the experience flooding out of her, running onto her thighs at her moment of release.

This rather intimate experience of live music was Naomi's secret thrill. She kept it that way, because no one had really understood quite how intense it was for her. Though she had tried, with several men.

"It makes you feel sexy, I can dig that." That was the usual type of reply, delivered with a shrug and a grin. When she tried to explain that it was more than just "feeling sexy," that it was actually like having sex-that it was enough to make her come with the slightest touch-the subject usually changed fast, because most of the men she'd met would rather believe it was their presence that was turning her on, rather than some extraneous factor. Maybe she was meeting the wrong type of man. She had hoped she would find someone who would understand her, someone who would play into it. Deep down she wanted to share it, like a sex toy or an aphrodisiac, but she'd come to the conclusion that she probably never would.

The nearest she had ever got to a true understanding was with a rock guitarist. He'd listened, curious, as she tried to explain it. He didn't say much-he never did-but he didn't dismiss the idea. So she had asked him to stand at the end of the bed and play for her. He had the look: long shaggy hair, stubble, sleazy in that don't-give-a-fuck rock musician way. She squinted her eyes, pretending she was at an actual gig, and watched him, letting the music take control. She got hot, really hot, unable to resist stroking her breasts and thrusting her fingers between her thighs. He'd loved it, watching her writhe across the bedcovers and masturbate while he played. Her fingers stroked her clit and she shoved two fingers into her wet cunt in time with the music. Riveted, he speeded his playing when he'd realized and she was quickly coming, moaning aloud and gyrating her hips against her hand. Abandoning the guitar, he unzipped his fly and dove onto the bed with her, bringing her back to a second climax by fucking her hard, really hard, banging her into the bed as if she was the drum and he was pounding out his very own fierce rhythm through her body.

It was good, damn good. Although she suspected the hot sex was more about his reaction to her "show" for him, than what the music did to them. It wasn't perfect, but near enough for her to get hopeful. Alas, when they went to the actual concerts together he preferred to schmooze, hanging out with the bands backstage then watching the live music from the side of the stage, hobnobbing with the other musicians. He'd tried to take her up there with him, but she'd declined, because that wasn't what she was after. She even told him about the wanking in the ladies', but that had just made him rush her back to his place, so he could get her flat on her back on his bed.

They'd shared several hot sessions with his guitar performance from the end of the bed, but now he was out there on a European tour somewhere, and she was back to trawling the music magazines for the perfect mix of music and venue. Like she had tonight. And what a night it promised to be. Whorl, one of her favorite ever bands, and The Academy, her favorite venue. The perfect combo beckoned to her.

She tagged on the end of the growing queue hugging the wall of the building. In the very early days, she used to come to these things with friends, but she had ended up frustrated. They all wanted to hang out together, somewhere where they could chat and watch, and get to the bar. What Naomi preferred to do was have a drink before she left home, and then forget all about that lesser form of self-indulgence. She had something better in mind.

When she got inside the venue she moved at will, seeking out her beloved bass pounding up through the floor. Before the band came on or between the bands, when the place was brightly lit, she kept on the move to avoid pickups. Standing near a crowd of people was also good cover and kept those achingly bad chat up lines at bay. There was no support band tonight, and that suited her well. The auditorium filled quickly, and she flitted about while the lights were up, anticipation running her ragged. Her heartbeat was already erratic, her core hot and her pussy tingling with anticipation.

It was a hot night and she'd dressed for comfort, Doc Martens, tight black vest and denim mini skirt, her hair loosely tied up on the crown of her head. When the final few sound checks were made, she began to rock along with the DJ music, noticing how it was chosen to lead into the bands set. The lights dropped, and the band emerged onto the stage-three guitarists, a drummer, and the singer, Carrie.

Naomi lifted her arms, clapping and cheering with the crowd, unable to keep the grin off her face. Carrie was wearing a short skirt not dissimilar to her own. Her blue-black hair flew out from side to side as she moved to the first beats of the drum. She was a small, sexy woman, overtly powerful. The men adored her. Some of them even tried to reach up on to the stage and touch her. She'd sometimes put her boot on their shoulders and kick them away, flashing her red underwear at them, blatantly. Naomi loved it, but very soon, when she found her own nirvana, she wouldn't even be noticing stuff like that.

The crowd surged forward and it was the time to stake her claim on a good spot. From experience she knew where the sound reverberated the most, weaving across the venue toward the spot. Skirting a pillar, she spied the place she wanted to be. There was a small gap in the crowd, enough for her to squeeze into. Focused on her target, she jumped when she bumped into another person, leaning up against the pillar. The crowd was moving at the other side of her, and she staggered. A strong hand reached out and grabbed her around her waist, steadying her. She looked into the man's face. He smiled, inclining his head.

Somewhat unnerved, she mouthed "thank you," to him. Even in the gloom, she could see that his eyes were narrowed as he quickly assessed her. He seemed to be alone. It wasn't very often that she saw another loner at a gig like this. She glanced back at the spot she was headed for. He followed her gaze and ushered her through, but when she looked back over her shoulder, he was still watching. The gig was under way, but after a few minutes she took another quick, curious look. Yes, he was definitely keeping his eye on her. He had short bleached hair, spiked and sexy. He caught her eye and returned her smile. Heat traversed her skin. His eyebrows were straight, decisive, almost mirroring his sharp cheekbones. With strong features and a quirk to his smile that suggested he was both cynical and adventurous, she couldn't help being aware of him. Normally she barely noticed the people around her. He was into the music as much as she was, moving to the sounds, his shoulders against the pillar seeming to ground him somehow. What a good idea, choosing that place to anchor himself. She couldn't help smiling, and made a note to try out the spot next time around.

The band moved into the second track, one of her favorites, and she was drawn back to the experience, moving her body, her eyelids lowering as she savored the music pounding through the floor. The sound soared out through the airwaves, wrapping around her before diving deep inside, teasing her most intimate flesh. God, it was so good. Each delivery of sound across the frets or drums might as well have been played on her erogenous zones. Her nipples were hard inside her vest. With every movement her body snaked, her thighs rubbing together as her hips swayed and dipped to the rhythm.

141

By the fifth track, her hair was beginning to escape its band, strands touching her shoulders. She swiped them away restlessly. As she did, she saw him looking over-the guy by the pillar. The stage lights swung over the audience, picking up his eyes, sharp and inquisitive. And he was watching her, watching with a knowing look in his eyes that felt as if he had touched her-like he knew exactly what she was feeling, and how she was feeling it. The lights moved and she danced on, enjoying the ongoing feeling of his eyes on her, even though she couldn't see them anymore, she could feel it. Heat pounded between her thighs, her pulse tripping. He knew how turned on she was, she was sure of it. She glanced back. Yes, even in the gloom she could see that he was still watching her.

Lifting her head, she focused on the stage. A moment later, she felt movement against her back, fingers resting on the curve of her hip. Her eyes closed, she breathed deeply. She didn't even have to look, to know. He'd made his way over. He knew.

"You really feel it don't you?"

The words were said close against her ear. Deviant pleasure shot through her, and her head dropped back in sudden ecstasy. Her hand reached over his where it rested on her hip, squeezing him in identification. Glancing back, she nodded. "All over me, and inside."

Moving closer, he spooned her hips inside his, swaying to the sound with her, feeling each rhythm and nuance, physically. They were locked into it, together.

"How did you know?" she asked.

He answered by hauling her closer still, and wedging her tight against him. She gasped when she felt how hard he was, the bulk of his cock against the crease of her arse through their clothes. Oh, but that was good. This is what she had wanted, a man who instinctively understood and played into the experience, and now the missing ingredient was right there, at her back, loaded and cocked for action. "This feels so good," she blurted.

He squeezed her waist in response, riding against her to the sounds. "Oh yes."

A heady thrill flared inside her when his hands roamed up and down her sides, stroking her body to the music. Her arms lifted as she swayed against him. His arms rose alongside hers, brushing against her with the hard sleek muscles of his biceps, enclosing her. Painfully aroused, she rippled in his grasp. He bent to kiss her neck. She groaned aloud, sensation snaking over her shoulders and back from the place his mouth had touched her.

"Come back to the pillar," he said. He nodded his head back at his previous viewing point.

She agreed and he took her hand, holding it tightly. A couple of people in the crowd look annoyed when they made their way back across their path, but she couldn't care. Her heart thudded while she watched him take up his position, pivoting his shoulders against the pillar so that his hips were right there for her to rest in. His booted feet were widely spaced, creating a niche between his legs for her to stand in. He smiled so wickedly that her mouth opened in anticipation, her breath catching her throat. She didn't know the guy at all, and yet she felt instinctively attuned to him because of this shared sexy appreciation of the live music. He patted his thighs, beckoning her closer, his intentions clear. He wanted to explore this too; he wanted them to feel it together. And so did she. She wanted to touch him again, to have his hands all over her; she wanted to know how far they could push it, right here in the crowd, right now. They were two people with a shared need-to experience each other in this place, in this moment.

Nestling into position, she reveled in the feeling of his strong, male body against her back. His aroused body. As his hands stroked over her hip bones, and then moved higher, to the soft underside of her breasts, her heart and mind beat out a fierce, direct response.

"Oh please, touch me, touch me everywhere," she said, unable to stop the words. She glanced back; unsure he'd even heard her amidst the layers of sound feeding out to them from the stage. But he smiled and moved against her, his head alongside hers, listening to her words as he watched the stage over her shoulder. She blinked and watched Carrie dancing across the stage, while his hands moved on her breasts, squeezing, molding the flesh. It sent a loop of fire from her nipples to her cunt.

"Play me, feel me," she urged. The words were tumbling out; she was losing control, desire overriding decorum. Her strongest physical need was sexual release. And he knew. She could see his response, the tightening of his mouth, the inhalation of breath, the subtle shift in his shoulders.

"Concentrate on the music," he said.

When she rested back, he had his hands on the waistband of her skirt immediately, with his fingers drumming against the zipper. Torturously close to her hot spot, and yet not close enough. She reached under his fingers, flipped open the button and lowered the zipper. He didn't even hesitate, sliding his hand inside the fabric, his fingers exploring her body. She moved against him, constantly aware of his erection, letting him know she was aware of it, too. His hand moved deeper, under the line of her underwear. With his hand in there, her underwear was pulled tight against her buttocks, stinging her, making her squirm. Her groin was pounding with need, her sex clenching and releasing. He clasped her pussy firmly, massaging it, lifting her in his grip. Her clit pounded, locked tight in between her sex folds. This time, her hips moved and it wasn't just the music, it was that and more- the sheer brutal need to feel that decisive touch on her clit.

144

Dizzy with deviant pleasure, she glanced about, watching the people moving around them. Any one of them could look their way, see them, point, or complain to security. But that somehow made it even hotter, dirtier and more dangerous. Right then he pressed deeper with one finger and it slid into her hot, damp niche. His finger was right over her clit, stroking it, and she couldn't have stopped him if she had truly wanted to. He was wanking her off, right there in the middle of the crowd. The music was in her blood, he was tuning into it and the thrill had her locked into the moment. Her body reacted, her head going back onto his shoulder, her shoulders pivoted against his chest. She reached her hand behind her back and squeezed the hard bulk of his cock through his jeans.

"Let me feel you in my hand," she said, when the sound dipped.

He looked at her, eyebrows raised, with a tight, wicked smile. He only hesitated a moment, then moved his free hand under her fingers. Undoing his zipper, he shifted and she felt the hot, silky surface of his erect cock against the palm of her hand. When she gripped and stroked it, he swore aloud and drew her in close against him, crushing her hand and his cock behind her back while he held and moved her with his hand locked over her pussy. His cock felt good, long and hard, the ridge around the head made her ache for it rubbing inside her, her sex clenching in response.

She was close, so close, her body trembling on the point of release. Then the music stopped, the band left the stage and the crowd began to chant clap and stamp their feet, trying to bring them back out for the encore. His hand latched ever tighter over her mons, crushing her clit, pushing her on. A sense of urgency got hold of her, time was short and she wasn't done yet. People were glancing around, chatting while they waited, and right there in the

145

crowd, the back of her skirt was riding up against her arse, the front zipper peeled open to give him access.

Dirty girl, she told herself. *Horny bitch.*

Her head lifted, a moan escaping her into the chants of the crowd. A sweet and sudden climax hit her and her body shuddered. Her thighs turned to jelly, her neck loosening and her head dropping forward.

By the time she had grounded herself, the guitarists were back on stage, playing furiously for the encore. Empowered, she pulled his hand free, turned in his arms and straddled one of his thighs, her hand clasping his cock again, stroking it swiftly as she looked up at his face.

The crowd roared. Carrie was obviously back on stage, but for Naomi it felt like it was for them, for their own performance. That thrilled her and she had to bite her lip to keep her in touch with the world outside of the music, and him. Soon they'd have to pull apart, but she wanted to make him come first.

When Carrie's voice lifted and started, she moved in regular, swift strokes. She could see the restraint in his expression, feel it walled up against her. They'd come this far, right there in the middle of the audience. She rubbed herself against his thigh, making the pleasure in her clit sparkle and last. "This is so good, you feel so good."

His eyes closed, his breath coming fast. His cock reached in her hand. "I'm going to come," he said urgently. He rested his forehead against hers. "If you don't stop, I'm going to come, right here."

"Don't stop," she said. She squeezed his cock massaging it fast, needing to trigger it, wanting to feel his release, wanting it all.

He locked eyes with her and she saw it coming there, his eyes blazing. His cock went rigid and he came, his shaft jerking, fluid running down between her fingers. Thrilled, she suddenly realized the crowd was cheering again and the music had stopped. The lights went up and he pulled himself together and acted fast, hauling her skirt straight, leveling her. Zipping his fly, he locked her against him again, holding her as if they were just having a post-gig hug. He grinned.

Her underwear was gloriously drenched, and she let out a breathy laugh as she looked at him, doing up her zipper and button while the crowd started shifting toward the exits. "I wish you'd been inside me," she murmured, her desires speaking for her-she wasn't even thinking about what she had said.

"So do I," he said with a hoarse laugh. He pushed her hair back from her forehead and kissed her mouth for the first time, softly now, curiosity in that intimate touch. With her hands on his chest, she could feel the both of them rushing on the experience, their hearts beating hard as they stayed against the pillar, the crowd shifting away on either side of them. As they drew apart, she studied him. In the light, his looks were maverick, and she saw how attractive his eyes were as he scrutinized her. She wanted him, she wanted to see him again, but right then she didn't want him to ask for her number, in case it spoiled the moment. She felt the question rising between them and went to put her fingers on his lips, but he caught her hand and rested it back on his chest. It made her want, and need, all over again and she rolled her hips into his.

"Are you going to be here for the Thursday night gig?" He lifted her hair from her shoulder as he asked, holding her with one hand around her hip as she moved against him.

He wasn't asking to see her again; he was asking to do this again. Pleasure rippled through her. "Yes," she replied without hesitation, not even pausing to consider who might be playing that night.

"In that case, I'll see you right here, on Thursday night." He stroked one finger down into her cleavage. "But, next time, don't wear any underwear." He reached to

147

kiss her again, his tongue moving slowly, languorously, against hers.

When he drew back, Naomi chuckled softly, her blood racing. "Improved access, hmm?"

He grinned. "I figure it could work-you wear heels; I'll bring a condom."

Now she was getting hot all over again, starting to squirm. "All the way? In the gig?"

He nodded, and pushed his fingers into her hair, tugging on it softly.

She grabbed him around the back of the neck and pulled him to her for one last kiss. "You're on," she stated as they drew apart. "I'll see you here, right here, Thursday."

As she strode out of the venue, she couldn't take the smile off her face, mentally calculating the hours until their next gig. Outside, in the street, the gig crowd clustered around the bootleg merchandisers and she weaved through them, heading to the tube station. Glancing over her shoulder, she looked up at the sign.

Live tonight.

The words were never truer.

THE THINGS THAT GO ON AT SIESTA TIME

Everything was quiet. It was mid-afternoon, siesta time. The sun smoldered across the crystalline-blue sky over Crete, sparkling off the Aegean Sea and making every rock, wall and tile glow. Sofia shielded her eyes and stepped quickly over the sun-baked rocks that led up to the back of the villa. She kicked off her sandals, stepped out of her uniform and sat down, resting her back against the shady wall behind her. The heat didn't bother Sofia, but the companion she was expecting was fair-skinned and needed the shade. *Lydia.* Lydia with the long legs and the big, baby blue eyes. Sofia's mouth watered just thinking about her.

There were so many advantages to working for the big-shot English movie producer. She got paid very well indeed, more than any maid in her village-a secluded backwash on the island, far from the tourist resorts where good jobs were more plentiful. The family was only going to be in the villa for a few months of the year, but intended to pay the staff all year round. The villagers were always eager for the gossip about who came and went at the big house and-best of all-she had access to the lovely Lydia, the daughter of the house.

Lydia had turned nineteen that year. She was fair and lithe, spoilt and incredibly naive. She pouted and preened, wandering around the grounds of the villa half-undressed, exposing herself in skimpy bikinis, shorts that frayed up over the cheeks of her cute behind and halter-necks tops that revealed the outline of her pert little breasts. Every man in the village lusted after the pretty English girl and a chorus of wolf whistles followed her whenever she rode her bicycle around the local area. Lydia clearly loved that kind of attention, but Sofia didn't think the little madam was helping herself any. Sofia was a very practical woman. She could see the attention made Lydia even hotter; her chaotic sexual chemistry swamped the entire household.

Sofia had watched as Lydia flirted outrageously with Stefanos and Nick, the grounds men. She lay on her sun lounger by the pool rubbing lotion into her bare limbs, flicking through trashy romance novels looking for the dirty parts. She'd pause and slip her shades down to inspect the men while they fished leaves out of the pool, eyeing their sleek muscled bodies at work. Those poor men were in a constant state of arousal with that little sex bomb on hand-so near, and yet so far out of their reach. Sofia smiled to herself and smugly treasured the fact that she'd had the first taste of the lovely Lydia that sultry summer.

She had discovered quite by chance that Lydia responded to both idle caresses and outright groping. Sofia brushed out Lydia's long blonde hair in the mornings and touched the soft skin of her neck and shoulders, stroking the flaxen strands down over her chest. Lydia gasped and whimpered, but didn't tell the maid to stop. Sofia murmured compliments, purring constantly and growling at the back of her throat whenever she made eye contact. When she helped her choose what to wear from the long walk-in wardrobe stuffed with clothes, Sofia got even bolder. She held things up against Lydia with cheeky hands, hands that molded the material in against her breasts and over her hips, both dexterous and suggestive. Lydia's body was programmed to respond. Riddled with frustration, she leached against the wily maid for more contact, staring at Sofia with wide eyes and open lips, whimpering, her breath constricted, while Sofia fondled her body through the skimpiest of barriers. Sofia knew Lydia could only hold out so long. She was a sexual time

150

bomb that was about to blow. Sofia grinned; she was getting nearer her target. She kept up that intrusive routine until there was such a plea in Lydia's eyes that it was obvious she had reached the point of desperation.

"Sofia," she declared. "You are touching me like a man would!"

"Oh, but you like it, yes." Sofia chuckled. Lydia's cheeks burned but she seemed unable to deny it. Sofia took her chance.

"Take off your robe," she whispered. "I am here to help you." Lydia obeyed. When she was naked Sofia dropped the dress she had held out in one hand and pushed Lydia back into the darkest recess of the wardrobe.

"You're so hot," she declared, squeezing Lydia's peaked nipples.

"That feels so good," she murmured, her body trembling with need. Sofia kissed her mouth to quiet the desperate moans of pleasure while she plundered Lydia's intimate flesh with knowing fingers. She had responded like a forest fire suddenly blazing out of control, hot, wild, desperate and clambering all over Sofia, even more responsive and willing than Sofia had guessed she might be, bucking wildly and crying at the point of her climax. High with the thrill of dominating the English girl and wet with wanting herself, Sofia stepped back, hoisted her skirt, squeezed her pussy lips hard, and then rubbed and flicked her clit, quickly, while Lydia stared at her lusty new lover with fascinated eyes. When she ventured to touch Sofia's sex, Lydia soon found her fingers crushed and her hand completely drenched.

From that point on the two young women ricocheted together in an almost constant cycle of arousal and fulfillment, each day bringing new games and pleasures. This was new for Lydia, but she was well and truly hooked.

This was their third time meeting outside. The spot was perfect; they were outside basking in the warm breeze and yet they were so secluded. The large flat rocks bedded in against the villa wall were overhung with honeysuckle and bougainvillea, shady and intoxicating. Sofia brushed the falling blossoms off her shoulder and pulled off her bra, her nipples growing hard and tingling at the sight of Lydia's lithe body hurrying over. She drew to a giddy halt, wisps of fair hair escaping from her ponytail, her aquamarine sarong wavering gently around her legs. She was breathless and flushed with arousal.

"Let me see you," Sofia whispered, lifting the hem of Lydia's sarong. She snaked one hand up around the calf of her leg, looking up at her from below. Lydia gasped and laughed, glancing over her shoulder back along the path behind her. She was still worried about discovery, but Sofia-being practical-reminded her it was siesta time. Besides which, Sofia's dark suggestions had an almost hypnotic effect on Lydia; she had no choice but to submit. She lifted the sarong, slowly revealing the curves of her inner thighs. Sofia watched with blatant, hungry eyes.

She was naked beneath, wearing just the bikini top and sarong. The mound of flesh at the juncture of Lydia's thighs was so softly rounded and firm that Sofia's mouth ached to bite the flesh and stick her tongue into the dewy niche.

"You are so wet, so ready?"

Lydia nodded vigorously. "I was getting so bloody horny, waiting in my room..." She untied the bikini top. Her breasts jutted forward, nipples the color of wine against the pale marble of her skin. Sofia pulled her down onto the flat rock, rolling over and quickly pinning her down. Lydia's head rolled from side to side, her legs opening.

"Hurry, before someone sees us," she declared, her eyes pleading with Sofia to be quick. Sofia smiled.

Sofia never rushed. The threat of being discovered would keep Lydia trembling on the point of climax, while Sofia gave her sweet torture with strokes of her tongue, mouth and fingers. Lydia shuddered and moaned; her lean body prone in submission.

"Every one is asleep..." Sofia rose up, pinning her friend down with her hands on her shoulders, and looked at her body with hungry eyes.

"For godsake, Sofia, do me..." she begged.

Chuckling, she lowered her head to trail her tongue over her belly and lower, warm breath moving the fair hair at her groin, the tip of her wet tongue parting the intimate folds. The inflamed morsel of her clit reared up between the plump, swollen folds of skin. She sucked then tongued the sensitive nub, stroking further down each time and sticking her tongue into the tight core of Lydia's sex. She sighed. She was in heaven there. Then a draft came up from somewhere and wafted the scent of flowers over them. Lydia's body grew still. A shadow had fallen over them. Sofia lifted her head. Lydia's expression was horror-struck as she stared over Sofia's shoulders

"Oh fuck it, I'm dead," she uttered, eyes closing.

Sofia turned. Stefanos was standing behind them. His eyes were glazed and he had a leering smile on his face. He was panting. Sofia's eyes dropped to his belt. His shorts were stretched tight over his crotch, a huge erection threatening to rip the fabric asunder. He'd been watching them and he'd got turned on. It served him right. Stefanos was a dirty spy. Why, just that morning she had spotted him watching her while she was doing her sweeping. He had stood on a box and peered over the edge of the terrace to look up at her from below. Sofia knew full well he was watching, but instead of shooing him off she bent over her task and hitched her skirt up around her hips, giving him a look at everything he was missing. Sofia never wore knickers. That was his punishment.

153

"Don't worry," she whispered. "He is coming here to us, not going into the house to tell." She soothed her friend, stroking her long hair back from her face. Then she spoke to him in Greek; he didn't speak any English. Stefanos laughed and nodded at her words, his thick black hair falling forward as he did so. "He wants, how do you say it, a piece of your action?" She nodded down towards the tumescent bulge below his belted waist.

"He wants me?" Lydia whispered, through fingers that covered her mouth and quelled her rapid breathing while she stared at the man. Sofia reached over and pulled Lydia's hand away from her face, kissing her gently on the cheek. She whispered in her ear.

"Yes, he wants you. Do you want to try him now? You've had one before right, a man?"

"Well, yes, once, and to be honest it was pretty crap, but the bloke didn't look anything like it. I mean him." Sofia patted her bottom approvingly. Stefanos was watching them, eagerly awaiting their reaction to his obvious intentions.

"You like it, yes?" Sofia chuckled. Lydia was staring, while she worked her thighs together, crushing her pussy lips; it was obvious she liked it. She nodded vaguely.

"Okay, I will tell him you want it and he can fuck you now." Sofia was a very practical sort. Lydia grew serious as she committed herself. She nodded again, eagerly.

Sofia asked him to show himself. She was having fun. She wanted to see Lydia with that big cock inside her. Stefanos was eager for it too. He unbelted his shorts before she finished the instruction to do so, dropping them to the ground and kicking them to one side, revealing the stout, long bough of his erect cock. He was huge and laden, his balls hanging heavily against his thighs. He was built like an ox. His cock twitched when both women stared at it. Sofia beckoned to him with her hand, pointing down to the largest flattish rock, the one where they had been lying together.

Sofia glanced at Lydia, whose eyebrows lifted in question. "He is ours." Sofia's eyes glittered with pleasure. She snatched at Lydia's hand, drawing her in. "You are ready?" Lydia nodded. His cock twitched again, its surface shiny and silken, a drop of dew resting at its very tip. "Climb onto him, as you would your bicycle, that way I can watch better." Stefanos moaned loudly when he realized they were negotiating positions. Sofia felt a pang of pity for him; he was quite obviously desperate for release and the horny action he'd been watching earlier had only made his problem that much bigger. His shaft was huge. Lydia hunched down beside him, then lifted one knee over his hips, coming to rest with her sex just above the broad head of his cock. She looked around at Sofia.

"Christ Sofia, help me, it's so bloody big," she whispered. Sofia beamed; to have the two of them so needy of her assistance was quite delicious in itself. Then, as she knelt down beside them, she felt Stefanos touching her hip. She looked down. He asked her to sit on his face. Her smile grew wide and her pussy filled with greedy anticipation. She straddled his head, facing Lydia. She lowered herself slowly onto his opening mouth. She began working herself against him, slowly at first, then more urgently. Lydia watched, eyes wide. When Sofia had found her rhythm she leaned forward and moved his erect cock towards the entrance of Lydia's plump, damp channel. The crown of his cock was so large that she had to ease it in very slowly, working the juices that oozed down against its hardness, to help its passage. It began to push inside Lydia. She whimpered; her body flexed and became taut, then her head went back in ecstasy, her hips moving forward to embrace the hard thing more vigorously when her body learned its measure. Sofia felt Stefanos stirring under her, responding to the twin pleasures. His mouth grew more

155

anxious on her intimate flesh, his tongue probing into her channel, strong and long, bringing on more liquid heat from inside her.

"Oh, my, it's so large," Lydia stuttered, gasping.

Sofia gave a throaty chuckle. "Press down, it will not harm you, precious one; enjoy him." Lydia's eyes closed and Sofia watched her riding the rigid column of flesh. A perverse sense of pleasure traveled through her as she watched and felt all at once. Lydia looked almost ready to collapse with pleasure and she began to plunge faster. Sofia suddenly felt a pang of envy; the crown of that magnificent cock must feel so good, buried in deep. She could see each exquisite spasm reflected in the expression on Lydia's face. Then, suddenly, she felt Stefanos buffeting her pussy lips more vigorously, thrusting his tongue faster, teeth nipping at her clit as he began to buck beneath her. Lydia let out a yowl of extreme pleasure, her body shuddering with release.

His body was taut with submission. Even if she hadn't have known that he was coming by the way his face moved distractedly against her flesh, she saw it ride up in Lydia's body-the renewed tenseness in her hips, her mouth a delectable open circle, a low moan in her throat. She wrapped her slender arms around herself and rocked on him, as if savoring the feeling.

A few moments later both women hauled themselves up and looked down at him. His breath was ragged. He was distracted, his expression vague, his eyes barely open.

Sofia smiled

"Look, his cock is beautiful, let's enjoy him for as long as we can," she said, her voice a whisper, the pounding inside her core barely relenting. Lydia nodded, transfixed by the stretch of strong male flesh. They moved either side of him. Sofia kissed his face, licking her cream from his cheeks. He was strong and smelt good, like he'd been helping himself to the master's cologne. Lydia fondled his thighs, while Sofia's curious hands roved over his chest and slid down the line of dark hair that guided her to the plumage that sprang in his groin. Her fingers settled there and stirred. He moaned in delight, undeniably pinned by their dexterous fingers on his body.

She looked down at his cock. It was beginning to become erect again. There was only one thing a practical woman could do. She reached for it, stroking it as it began to grow quicker in her hand. The power of it growing beneath her fingers affected her. She preferred playing with women, but she felt needy and wild with this thing in her hand. Her pussy ached for it. The shaft was rigid now, hot, and ready. She wanted to feel its strength inside her body, just as Lydia had. She bent down and kissed its swollen tip and then tasted his essence with her tongue, sweeping over the firm, soft surface in circular movements. A thread of urgency flew round her blood, she was desperate: he was more than ready to be mounted again. She climbed onto him and when she had taken him to the hilt she groaned. It felt so very good, she could hardly move. Then she began riding him, hard and fast. She was close to flooding.

His chest arched up towards her, his rib cage jutting, his neck a line of tensed muscle. His eyes begged her for his second release. The swell and throb of his pulsating rod was so insistent, her flesh began to melt and shift around it. His fingers fumbled where he entered her body, stroking at the point where their flesh met, the cup of his hand latched over her swollen clit. Sofia was impressed. Her pussy clutched at him, rhythmic and intense, then spasmed. She bit her lip to stop herself from screaming aloud. His eyebrows drew down and Sofia felt the line of muscle that stretched from his hip down the front of his thighs tighten and reach beneath her. Her body was lifted up with its strength. When he came it was with mighty, Herculean lunges.

The end of siesta time was near.

The three revelers began to dress quickly. Sofia smiled, like a cat with all the cream. She'd sampled the goods and enjoyed them. She told Stefanos that if he kept quiet he could come back for more. With him involved their games were going to be even better: the possibilities were endless.

"Are you sure he's not going to tell anyone?" Lydia asked.

"I think he will keep the secret so that he can have some more of it now and next summer, when you come back to us." She smiled at Lydia. "Also, I can think of at least one way to keep him quiet, in between." She turned to Stefanos and waggled her tongue at him, winking. He grinned back at her. She had decided that she liked him, after all, and-being a practical sort-she knew she would need something to keep her warm through the long winter months ahead.

IT'S JUST NOT CRICKET

Mad dogs and Englishmen go out in the midday sun. Ella usually avoided it all costs, but the lure of Lord Findlebury's charity cricket match was strong. Ella was a huntress by nature, and sometimes huntresses are forced to go out at daytime as well as at night. It wasn't the sport but the players that interested her. Ella had a dominant sexual disposition and a taste for languid aristocratic types. She loved the idea of them swooning under her while she rodgered them senseless. The very thought of it was enough to make her blood rush and get her underwear hot and sticky within moments. Put plain and simple, Ella wanted to fuck the aristocracy.

It was her little secret. Jilling off to old videos of Brideshead Revisited wasn't the sort of the thing you announced to your girlfriends, now was it? The opportunity to pursue her dream presented itself quite unexpectedly, one hot August day at the office, when she heard Jacinta chattering from the other side of her cubicle. She only half listened, but when she heard mention of Lord Findlebury's sponsored cricket match being held on the village green at Fossett, she reached into her drawer for her box of choccies. Assuming a friendly smile, she stood up and offered the box over the wall of the cubicle.

Jacinta and her cohort squealed in response to her sudden appearance over the partition.

"Help yourself to a chocolate."

Jacinta's eyes lit up. Jacinta loved chocolate.

Ella chattered appropriately. She told them how she adored the countryside and the thrill of the cricket season. Within the time that it took the three of them to clear one tray of chocolate she elicited an invitation to join

Jacinta at the forthcoming annual cricket event. Ella was triumphant. That night she went home and treated herself to an expensive bottle of red wine and a Rupert Everett video bonanza, whilst mounting her favorite dildo, repeatedly.

Sunday arrived. It was a steaming hot day, the city pavements sizzled. The roads were packed with cars heading for the coast, the occupants sweltering inside. Didn't they know they'd be baked before they reached their destination? People did weird things in the heat, she warned herself. Brits just aren't used to it. She liked to be cool and in control. In temperatures like this she'd usually be at home reading a good book under a fan, until dark. But the event of the day had a powerful draw and she drove out of London and into the greenbelt with a heady sense of anticipation, air vents on full blast.

Fossett was a pretty little village on the border of Kent and Sussex, picture-postcard perfect. In the summer heat haze it looked as if Vaseline had been smeared on the lens, all soft focus and idyllic. She parked up, straightened her outfit-she was dressed to the nines in garden party attire; strappy high heels and a floating, gauzy dress that threatened to slope down off the shoulders at any given moment-then located the village green and met with Jacinta.

The cricket match had already started and her sense of eagerness almost overwhelmed her efforts to be polite. She just about managed to acknowledge Jacinta's introductions to her gawky friends, before quickly installing herself in a deckchair with a glass of fizz. She then focused herself entirely on the job at hand: assessing the loping men on the pitch with an expectant, hungry gaze.

How could anyone think that rubbing a ball over their hip in that manner was anything but sexual? She contemplated the conundrum, with a self-indulgent smile.

She compared their techniques. Several of them gave the ball a fast rub and a blow for luck, before launching it. That was cute, but rather too quick. No, she preferred the men who toyed with the ball at great length while they checked out the field, and then rubbed it, long and slow, as they made a loping approach to their shot. The player who was the master of the preferred technique was a tall, lanky fellow with a heavy flop of dark hair that he occasionally swept back from his forehead. When *he* rubbed the ball on the front of his whites, he did it with such exquisite nonchalance that Ella was hooked.

She began to follow his actions, and his actions alone. She noticed with pleasure that he was completely lacking in self-consciousness. Lean and elegant, he resembled the splendidly handsome Jeremy Irons. After just a few minutes, he became her target and as a result she grew hotter by the moment. She pictured herself hauling off the target's shirt, revealing the skin of his leanly muscled chest. She could just see him, reclining against the banisters on the cricket pavilion, while she bound his arms back, to render him helpless to her onslaught.

She sighed deeply. Another glass of bubbly had found its way into her hands. She pictured herself opening his fly, holding his cock in her hand, weighing it in assessment; she could almost hear him begging her to use him and use him well. She crossed her legs, her sex pounding with need. A bead of sweat tickled between her breasts-she stroked it with an idle finger. She massaged her thighs together, savoring the sparks that emanated from her hot, aroused flesh.

"Time."

The umpire's call rang out across the green. Ella was forced to abandon her reverie when she realized that the game had stopped for refreshments. It was early afternoon. People began to get up and move around. The men had started to head in their direction. Action was required. She stood up from her deckchair. When she moved, it was like walking into a sauna. She ruffled her hair out across her shoulders and made sure she had plenty of eye-catching cleavage on display. The target was heading straight for them.

"Jacinta, darling," he called out. "What a good girl you are. I see you've brought us some top-notch totty." He grinned in the direction of Ella's cleavage, while rubbing his cricket bat in a very lewd manner.

Totty? What a bloody cheek. She wasn't "totty," she was sophisticated, she was in control. She flushed with annoyance and glared back at him.

"Oh, Freddie Findlebury," Jacinta called back across the green. "Do be careful, we can see your prick standing to attention from here."

Ella's jaw dropped. *Dear God, they were positively uncivilized.* She was expecting polite conversation. *Restraint.* She couldn't help noticing that Jacinta was right, though. As he got closer, she found her gaze magnetized to the decidedly impressive package outlined in his expensive white linen pants.

"I saw you watching me, you saucy little tart." He spoke directly to her. Indignation flared through Ella's veins. She was the one who did the come-ons. He was supposed to be languid. Submissive. Before she managed to pull herself together and reply, he returned his attention to Jacinta.

"I hope you'll be bringing your little friend back to the estate."

"I will, if you like." Jacinta seemed completely unfazed by the man's attitude, but Ella watched the exchange with a growing sense of bewilderment. The estate? He must be Lord Findlebury's son. She'd only gone and eyed up the top aristo on the scene. Despite the nature of their encounter, she had to congratulate herself on that one. It was uncanny. However, his behavior bore little resemblance to the screen heroes that she had been fantasizing about.

She watched him with blatant curiosity as he sauntered towards the tea tables. He'd stirred up a very confused mix of emotions. He was rude and presumptuous, but the fact that he'd responded to her was a real turn-on. He'd also extended some sort of invitation for later, and he had given her a clear signal that he was interested. She swiped back her hair. The heat was getting to her. She'd have to level her head.

After a cup of Earl Grey and some consideration, Ella decided that she was reasonably content with developments, especially because she felt sure that she could put a stop to his cheeky attitude through the use of extra bondage. She preferred not to gag her men because she liked to hear them beg, but she admitted that it might be necessary with Lord Motor Mouth here.

She fanned herself with a magazine and managed to slow down on the booze intake during the next innings. Occasionally he glanced over, as if to see if she was still around. She darted her glance away, but couldn't contain her smiles. At the end of the match Jacinta gave her instructions to follow the procession of cars for the after-match party. Ella sat behind the wheel of her car, humming with excitement. The day had already far exceeded her expectations, and if she was correct in her observations, Freddie hadn't been giving anyone the eye but her.

"Wow," she murmured, when the procession began to park up along a driveway that opened out in front of an impressive manor house. She pulled her car in behind the others, and took time out to refresh her make up. "Ammunition," she declared, as she topped up her lipstick.

The cricket match was obviously the big community event of the year. A large proportion of the

match attendees had migrated with them. Thankfully the
heat mellowed out around the house, where plants trailing
over the arbors gave cover and the gardens were still damp
from the sprinklers. Ella wandered in and around the
throng, sucking in the ambience with a self-satisfied smile.
It was almost as if she'd been beamed onto the set of a
costume drama-how could she not love that?

Lord Findlebury sat in state, on the terrace, the
older visitors gathering around him to chatter. In a gazebo
in the gardens, an eccentric looking bunch of musicians
played acid jazz. Freddie was the perfect host, moving
casually from one clique to the next, offering a word of
encouragement or calling over to the waiter to bring more
drinks. He stopped to oversee the barbecue. Hungrily, Ella
watched him flipping over steaks on the grill. It wasn't
food that she was eyeing up.

He winked at her. Oh yes, he was interested all
right. She knocked back another flute of wine. The power
was within her grasp. She'd have him begging for it in no
time. She turned on her heel and headed off into the
gardens, where a maze of high hedges gave shade from the
heat and the damp ground gave way underfoot. Glancing
back, she could see that he followed. *Just like a little puppy
dog.* She smiled, congratulating herself, moving deeper into
the maze.

"You're really up for it aren't you, you saucy
wench."

Ella gasped when he appeared around the corner
of the tall laurel hedge in front of her. He must have gone
a different route to head her off at the pass. How
annoying.

"My name is not saucy or wench, it is Ella, and
I'm not interested in your bloody cheek. Just because you
own the manor you can't have everything you want."

She suddenly noticed that he was even better
looking up close, and a little older than she had previously

thought. He was well over six feet tall. He'd pushed up the sleeves of his shirt, revealing surprisingly strong, well-muscled forearms. He laughed in response to her retort and the sound had a deep, satisfied timbre.

"Don't be coy, Ella dear, it doesn't suit you."

She bit her lip. Annoying as it was, he was probably right on that score; coyness was not a characteristic she would wish to claim. Moreover, the fact that he had recognized that in her stirred something primal inside her, something fierce and power hungry. Had she met her match?

"I'll call for help, if you dare to touch me." She lifted her chin, defiantly, challenging him. She felt the urge to do battle, to the little death.

Even if she meant it, would anyone even hear or respond? The faint sounds of acid jazz still reached them, but the chatter of the party was barely discernible out there. His eyebrow flickered, his pupils dilating. He was unmistakably aroused by her attitude. The more she stood up to him, the more he took it as a challenge. He stepped closer, into the shade, then stroked one finger through her hair and down one shoulder. The intimate action sent wild darts of arousal skittering beneath the surface of her skin.

"You came here looking for a right good seeing-to, and I intend to give it to you."

Ella's mouth opened in indignation. "You don't know what I came here for, you bloody prig." She was smarting. She couldn't have been that obvious, surely not? Besides, the need that he had kindled inside her had become truly urgent, and she wasn't about to give in to him that easily.

She stared up at him, unsettled because his face was cast in shadow. She couldn't judge his intentions. Could she make a dash for it? Did she want to? Time stood still. She could hear insects, the distant music wavering on the atmosphere, her own heartbeat. Warm air

165

funneled down the corridors of the maze, like a sirocco. It was seductive, suggestive. It was like a license to act crazy. She bent and quickly unlatched her sandals, grabbing them into one hand as she set off, barefoot, at top whack.

"A filly with spirit!"

She heard his declaration as she lurched off, as fast as her feet could carry her. *Filly*? Where did he get off thinking of her in those terms? She was disgusted. At least, Ella thought she was. Freddie roared as he set off after her. She squealed, weaving in amongst the bushes, her heart pounding.

When she felt that she had made some time, she glanced over her shoulder. He was nowhere in sight. She laughed triumphantly and headed for the cover of a wooden hut set behind one of the tall laurel hedges. Her breath rasped in her lungs, her blood rushing. She felt thoroughly elated by the chase and by the fact that she was outrunning him.

That was when she tripped and fell.

She managed to get to her knees, cursing when she heard her dress ripping, before she heard his footsteps thundering up behind her. His hands snatched at her ankles. He jolted her back towards him and she fell flat on the ground. He hauled her legs apart. Warm air surged up between her thighs. Her sex prickled with a delicious sense of anxiety. It was torturous. She was creaming.

"Let me go, you beast!"

Freddie flipped her over, easily. "I'll let you go when I'm convinced you're not gagging for it." There was a challenge in his eyes that she found it hard to meet. "Your nipples are like totem poles, my dear, you're ripe for it and you know it."

Could she even deny that? Humiliation swept over her and, much to her surprise, she found that it was as if pure delirium had been released into her veins. She was unable to reply. It's the heat, she reasoned, shocked at herself.

He had her pinned down, kneeling astride her hips, with both her wrists captured above her head in one strong hand. "Perfect," he said, grabbing at the door of the nearby hut with his free hand. He reached inside and pulled out a handful of green metal loops mounted on sharp prongs.

"What the hell is that?" Ella asked, genuinely freaked.

Freddie gave a dark laugh. "Anyone for croquet?" he declared, as he spread-eagled her and pinned her to the ground at wrist and ankle with the croquet hoops. He pushed the prongs deep in the ground, his whole body weight behind them.

Fuck. It was nothing like being in a costume drama after all; it was more like being on a bloody army assault course. She tried to move when he sat back on his haunches to admire his handiwork, but she was well and truly fixed to the spot. Not only that, but she found that the more she wriggled, the further her dress slipped up and over her hips, exposing her thighs and the scrap of black lacy G-string twisting over her groin.

He chuckled at her efforts to break free.

"Shut up or someone will hear you," she said, through gritted teeth.

"I thought you wanted to be rescued." He smirked at her. He pulled out his cock and lazily massaged it in one fist while he gazed down at her spread legs. He was impressively erect, making her sex contract with need. She squeezed her eyes shut. She was totally helpless. There was nothing she could do but submit to him. Strangely enough, the realization unleashed a rush that threatened to overwhelm her. She couldn't, she couldn't lose control, not like this. It would be too humiliating. She strained against the hoops, but it was futile.

Freddie looked calm and focused. That made her wriggle all the more. He reached over to her hips and tore the G-string in two, hauling the shreds down the length of her legs. It was sudden and shocking.

"Very nice," he murmured, looking appreciatively at her exposed pussy.

Ella groaned. The intimation was too dirty, too direct, but for some reason it set her on fire. He climbed over her, and then leaned down to kiss her, his tongue probing into hers. That made it so intimate, so real; she felt stripped raw. Excitement thundered over her.

"Keep still," he ordered, when her body lurched up against his. She could smell his body, hot and male. He rubbed his cock back and forth against her clit, making her gasp with pleasure. He teased her with it, grinning down at her when she whimpered with painful pleasure. Then he was inside her, his blood pounding inside hers. Her hips were angled to take him in, her flesh melting onto the hard, hot shaft.

Fuck it, that felt so damned good!

"Christ, you're wet," he uttered, and rammed inside her.

Ella was helpless, totally helpless. She cried out in ecstasy, her head falling back. He moved his face into the curve of her neck, his mouth sinking against her skin. When her warm, wet sheath clutched at him, it sent torrents of sensation through them both. He drew back, and then reached further inside, each internal jolt freeing a demand for more. She rose up within her restraints and tried to match his rhythm. Their eyes were locked, urging each other on in the quest. Ella struggled for breath, silently pleading for more. She was going to come, damn it. She was submitting, and God it felt good! Her hands fisted within the hoops, her sex beginning to spasm.

He fought for the release, his hips jerking frantically. He was so very deep; he struggled with it to last, or be finished. She contracted, tightening on his throbbing cock; then his hands were on her hips, holding her pressed down hard and tight as he thrust fiercely for the prize. She gave a deep moan, surfacing through her ecstasy. "Don't move," he instructed.

She obeyed, watching him, still panting.

He pushed one hand between them, arresting her throbbing clitoris with the stroke of his thumb, the stem of his cock inside the curve of his fingers. She cried out in ecstasy, another sudden climax springing free from the pressure of his touch, inside and out. He gave her a dark smile, and then rammed his cock home. Her head jolted, her body snared, but clutching at his throbbing, distended cock, over and over. His body jerked mightily and he came in a sudden, dazzling rush that drew a curse from his lips.

"Fuck me, that was good," he eventually managed to murmur against her ear.

She didn't give him the satisfaction of qualifying her obvious pleasure in his attack. She had enjoyed it; she admitted it. To herself. Wasn't life strange, she reflected. Not at all what she had expected, but somehow entrancing all the same.

Freddie leaned up on one elbow to look at her, then kissed her quite tenderly as he climbed over her and tugged out the croquet hoops.

Once freed, she stayed put. "It's cool here, in the shade," she murmured, eyeing him. She wanted to linger.

"I agree, but I hear voices approaching. I'm protecting your honor."

He was right. Laughter. Damn. This was their spot. She sat up and began to tidy her hair with the practiced nonchalance of a true sexual libertine. He straightened her dress on her shoulder, planting a kiss on her neck.

"Can I have a repeat performance?"

Ella couldn't retain her smile. "Maybe...I'll think about it. The heat did bad things to me, I can't think straight now."

He growled. "If the heat did that to you I suggest we meet in Jamaica."

"Hey," she gave him a stern glance. "Next time we meet on my turf, where I can keep cool with my fan."

It had been delivered as a threat, but his eyes sparkled, his smile vibrantly suggestive. "The fan is allowed, as long as I'm control of where it's blowing." He glanced down at her pussy, where she was covering herself over with her dress.

She laughed. She rather liked this game. What would transpire? She could barely wait to find out, and neither could Freddie Findlebury.

HARVEST TIME

"Take me to bed," Ash rasped against her hair, clutching at her.

"And me," Joel growled, pressed against the other side, the three of them clinging together, breathless and panting, in the gloom of the hallway. Joolz threw back her head, laughing joyously, reveling in the sensations. They had chased each other back across the moonlit fields and tumbled into the cottage in the early hours, giddy after a night of festivities unique to Dorset villages in harvest time.

She dropped her sandals from her hand and led the men to the large bedroom, peeling off her dress as she went. It was still hot, even though it was so late; it was easily one of the hottest summers she could remember.

"I'm sticky as hell; I'm going to take a shower," she said.

Joel threw himself into a chair, ruffling his hand through his spiky black crop, eyeing her hungrily. Ash, lean and fair, with a goatee beard and shaggy hair, lounged on the bed, arms behind his head, watching her through narrowed eyes as she dropped the dress on the floor and then turned away into the adjacent bathroom.

Joolz smiled at her reflection in the bathroom mirror as she flicked on the shower, enjoying the anticipation that had hummed between them all evening. They were three college friends who had fallen into a relationship quite casually, a few weeks earlier. First Ash and Joolz had become lovers, and then one night Joel had been with them, and he'd stayed and he'd kissed her while Ash fucked her. She'd put her hand on Joel's cock, jerking him off, and it had sent Ash wild. That night he gave her the best fuck she'd ever had, rutting at her like a wild man.

After that, the three of them hung out together even more, constantly wired for sexual suggestion. Sometimes the men took her one after the other; sometimes she liked to watch one man wanking, while the other fucked her. The two men let Joolz determine the mechanics of their relationship. That amused her; they didn't like that kind of responsibility, but she did, so it was a very satisfactory arrangement. Joolz enjoyed the power. She also enjoyed slowly upping the ante between them.

She soaped her breasts under the lukewarm water, smiling as she thought back to the image of the men in the pub, how lean and gorgeous they looked alongside the beefier farm workers. The two men noticed when other men looked at her, their gaze darting and suggestive. Ash seemed to take a perverse kind of enjoyment from sharing her with Joel, and it made him want her in a very forceful, physical way. Seeing Ash get territorial and act on it made Joel hot. He told them it was like watching a live sex show of his very own. And Joolz? Joolz simply enjoyed each and every experience the dynamic between them offered.

That evening, while a fiddler played in the snug. and skittles led the gambling in the main bar, they had both held her and kissed her. Amidst the celebrations of fecund mother earth, it was as natural an occurrence as the rising of the seasons. The three London socialites had found that the traditions of the countryside inspired something even more earthy and real, something entirely unashamed. They had claimed her as theirs, publicly.

Joolz flicked her hair back as she climbed out of the shower, glancing around at the old bathroom walls, remarking to herself how well the place had stood up to time. She hadn't been back to the rambling cottage for four years, even though it remained in the family after Grandma had passed on and was always on offer for holidays. It was the place where she had spent her childhood summers and big family celebrations at Christmas time and other special times, she reflected. She'd slept with Laurence, here. He was her first lover. She glanced back at the mirror, remembering. Her dark eyes turned black, her mouth opening as thoughts spiraled in her mind. Back then she'd been eager, but jittery. Now, she looked ripe, ready. After a few moments, she lifted her kimono from the back of the bathroom door and slipped it on.

A wedge of moonlight carved into the room from the open curtains. They were both sitting on the bed, expectantly. They looked at her body through the flimsy silk kimono she had thrown on. It was sheer and clung to her damp skin. She shook her head and her long chestnut hair tumbled over her shoulders, damp from the shower.

"You like nubile, half undressed in the moonlight," Joel said, from the bed, smirking as he pulled his t-shirt over his head. Joolz smiled and wandered towards them. She crept up from the bottom of the bed to lie between them.

"That's funny that you said that, you know," she mused. "Because I'd just remembered that I lost my virginity in this very room."

"Mmm, Joolz. You say all the right things." Joel rolled closer and lifted up on his elbow, moved his mouth to her ear lobe, and kissed it, his hand stroking over her breast.

"Really?" Ash asked, looking at her with curiosity. "Tell us about it," he prompted. She smiled. It turned him on, big time, when she talked about sex. He put one hand on her thigh, gently enclosing its curve of flesh as he climbed next to her. Joel began to unbutton his jeans, kicking them off.

"I was eighteen. It was a colleague of my Father's, Laurence. I haven't seen him in years." Her mind drifted

173

back and forth, riding the time between then and now. "I'd been infatuated with him for an age. He was well aware of it and he-well, he pursued me." She gave a light laugh.

"That's understandable," Joel said. "The guy obviously had good taste." He chuckled, kissing his mouth against her silk-draped breast. She covered his head with her hand, stroking his hair.

"Go on," Ash said, his eyes dark with lust and a spark of something else. Envy? Joolz lifted her eyebrows at him, a teasing smile lifting the corners of her mouth.

"He'd just come back from Nepal, where he'd been writing a travel journal. I was swept up in the visions he described during dinner. At the end of the evening, when I left, he kissed my hand. Deliberately. It made me feel like a woman, I suppose. The second night of his visit, he retired early and when I went to bed, I found him in the corridor. He caught me in his arms and put his fingers to his lips. Then he pulled me in here." Joolz glanced round the room. Joel was kissing her shoulder; tiny light nibbles, just anchoring her.

"He asked me questions about my sexual desires, and I told him about the strange tugging that I felt, every night, the unfulfilled lust, deep inside. He began to stroke my body, slowly taking my clothes off."

Joel shifted against her, responding to her comments. She felt his hard outline against her thigh. Her sex had begun to cloy with need, need inspired by real sensation, and memory.

"Then he began describing what it felt like, for him, wanting me ...he told me he wanted to push his cock deep inside me. His fingers were all over my underwear, pulling it off me. I could barely breathe." Joolz paused. Ash had risen and stripped of his shirt, baring the strong lean muscle of his chest. She linked one finger over the belt on his jeans, tugging it open. She looked up at him, provocatively; as she popped open the buttons on his fly.

"Go on."

"He explored me thoroughly with his fingers; all I could do was let the experience eat me up-his eyes were so inquisitive on my virgin flesh. But I wanted him to look at me..." She drew his cock out in her hand, embracing it firmly as it grew even harder in her hand. He groaned, his body wavering.

"I want to look at you, now," Joel commanded, his hand roving up her thigh. Ash reached over and stopped him.

"Let her finish," he whispered, through clenched teeth. The hunger had bitten him. Joolz smiled but looked away as he stripped and lay back against her again, his body taught with lust. .

"I was a bit...scared-when he undressed and I saw his cock. I hadn't seen a real man naked before...only pictures." Ash jammed his cock against her side, his eyes glazed, his features contorted with restraint. She squirmed against him; he locked one hand over her hip, holding her against his pulsing cock. "He led me to the bed and spread my legs wide." She gestured towards the end of the bed, her feet sliding against one another as she saw herself there.

"He kissed me down there, first, not deeply... like you do." She paused to stroke Joel's head again. He muzzled against her. "But enough to make me whimper. When he touched me inside, I thought I would die. It was excruciating, but so good! Then, his cock. It felt huge, so huge. I wondered how I could ever manage it, but at the same time, I wanted to impale myself on it. To have it thrust-thrust right through me."

Joel groaned, his body writhing alongside hers. He lifted open her kimono, stroking her bare legs. She opened them in response.

"Touch me," she said, turning to him. His fingers slid against the wetness of her sex folds.

175

"Go on," Ash murmured, his body extended against hers, his mouth brushing her neck. "Don't stop." His erection was rigid. He pressed it against her thigh. Joolz gasped, completely aware of the male forces surrounding her, and still picturing herself spread-eagled on the bed, breathless and afraid, taking the huge cock inside her for the first time. She closed her eyes and let the feeling of Joel's fingers questing through her wetness take her back again. She wanted penetration.

"I wanted-penetration. I wanted it, but it also terrified me. When he began to take me I thought my body would break, he seemed so huge. But, God, it felt good!"

Joel rammed his fingers inside her; she gasped, and then began to move on them, her head falling back, her body shifting against the bed.

"He fucked me so hard, mercilessly."

Ash knelt up, dragged her legs wider apart, and climbed between them. He pulled Joel's hand away from her, his cock quickly finding the wet niche between her legs. Joolz cried out, a muted scream, as he thrust inside her.

"Shut up!"" he ordered. "Not another word." His body drew back and reached. He was wild; it was as if he was suddenly furious at her words, and at the heat she was giving off. "Don't say another word, Joolz." He gritted his teeth as he thrust inside her. Oh, that was good. A demon sprang up inside her.

"Harder than that ... Ash, he rode me harder than that." She held him with her eyes, urging him on, the challenge in her words. He rode up against her, thrusting repeatedly, more quickly, fiercer. Joolz was swept up into his rhythm, molten inside, sensitized to every movement.

Ash thrust faster, rose up on his arms, and then freed a bitter cry of anger in his throat as his cock came suddenly, spurting into her. He had barely slowed his movement and Joel was there, ready to take her from him.

Joolz felt a rush of departure, and then she was filled again. Two cocks, she was having two cocks, one after the other. The men with her and those in her memory a multitude of pleasures, already she was blossoming into orgasm. Her pelvis was awash with heat, her body shuddering.

"I want more," she cried out. Joel swore under his breath and fucked her harder, even while she was still clutching him.

"You look so bloody hot when you come," Joel whispered. Her core pounded, waves of relief washing over her.

"I want more," she cried out again, delirious with pleasure. Her eyes flickered open when she heard Ash's voice.

"Don't come, not yet," he said, his hands on Joel's shoulders. Joel swore again, louder. The physical effort of halting, when every atom in his body wanted to go on, demanded all his efforts. Ash was standing beside the bed, fisting his cock, which was already long and hard again, ready for more. "She said she wants more, she wants more cock." Ash's eyes were flashing. Joel pulled out for a moment. Holding his aching balls tight, he sat back onto his haunches, pressing against the base of his cock to hold back from coming. Ash moved closer, offering his cock to her. Joolz turned her face into it. Oh, yes. She wanted to feel it fill her mouth; she wanted to taste his passion.

"Do you still want more?" Ash asked her, his voice controlled. Joolz groaned, her body ricocheting with a riot of opposing signals; she was unable to form words. "Yes," he murmured, and she nodded her head, her hair trailing over her face as she swayed, intoxicated with it, overwhelmed with shame, shame that flooded her sex when she was forced to concede that she did want more.

"Yes, two cocks, I want you to fill me up," she blurted out, moving round so that her head was hanging back at the edge of the bed, opening her mouth to him.

177

"Sweet Jesus," Joel said, pressing harder still.

Ash's cock was close to her lips, still slick and oozing, a drop of come weeping out onto the swollen dark-red head. He drew back and Joolz cried out, grabbing at him, thrusting him into her mouth, suckling hard. He stood directly behind her and slid deep against her throat with each slide in and out of her mouth. Joolz wanted it, but she wondered if she could take it without gagging, if she could breathe at all. Then she found her rhythm, swallowing a good length of him and an intake of breath on each of his thrusts. She felt Joel's hands on her again, urgent, and the nudge of his cock in her sex. She wanted this so badly, she wanted to be filled and used, to be taken every way, so full of cock that every ounce of her was going to be drenched with come.

"That's it," Ash whispered, panting. "Oh yes, you're so good at that." He rubbed his hand over her breasts, examining her, his fingers hard against her peaked nipples. Joolz felt feverish, weak and agitated all at the same time. She was so thoroughly pinioned and exposed. Waves of sensation skittered over her whole body. It felt thoroughly debauched, but right and true, as if being subdued and penetrated by them both like that was what her body craved in that moment. She felt like mother earth herself, rooted through and penetrated with virile roots spilling their seed on her land. Her body went limp, malleable, absorbing each wave of sensation. She began to come again, very quickly, her body lifting up, her sex clenching and spasming.

Ash grunted, his body gleaming with sweat and taut with effort, his hips rolling. Joel was panting, his cock rock hard, at its most swollen as it finally shot its load. Ash cursed loudly; then his cock began to jerk: once, twice, three times, giving her the taste of him, before he pulled out, still spurting furiously over her neck and breasts. He leaned over her, panting, and when she caught her breath again, she pulled him down onto the bed with them, dizzy with pleasure.

"Enough cock, Madame?" he asked, his voice edged with sarcasm.

"Enough-for now," she retorted.

"You're insatiable," Joel murmured, collapsing back on the bed.

"Not with you two around." She chuckled.

"Well, if this Laurence friend of yours should drop 'round," Ash mused, as he lay down and kissed her forehead, affectionately. "I think we should tie you to the bed and show him how to really fuck a woman."

"Oh, now there's an idea," Joolz said, smiling. She had to admit, the suggestion fascinated her. "But he might just drop 'round anytime, so you should get ready to act on that threat of yours."

Ash's head jerked up and he looked at her, possessively. Joolz flickered her eyebrows at him, hauling him closer.

"Just teasing."

"Sure you are," he replied, and they looked into each other's eyes, the suggestion he had made taking root. With Joel at her back, the three of them began to drift towards sleep, limbs entwined, sticky, and happily sated. For now. Joolz smiled to herself; tomorrow she might just have to up the ante again. One important lesson that she had learned from the countryside was that you made your hay while the sun shined, then you were sure to be kept well stocked, and satisfied, all year around.

SASKIA WALKER

RAPT

For a split second, I thought it was snowing. But no, it was rain, as usual. The snow never comes to England much before January, which is just as well because as a nation we don't know how to deal with it, and right now I didn't want to be stuck in gridlock traffic due to an unexpected flurry of snow on Christmas Eve. I braced myself for the cold drizzle and stepped out of the Heathrow European arrivals terminal, wondering how long I'd have to wait for a taxi.

As I darted toward the taxi rank, I threw a filthy look down at the laptop bag I had in one hand and the bulging gift bags in the other. Who sent their journalists on long distance assignments on Christmas Eve? Only my boss! And because I hadn't been organized enough to get the presents sorted and delivered the weekend before, they'd had to come with me on the trip. All I wanted to do was go back to my apartment, get out of my heels and my business suit, and have a nice long bath... and some serious sexual relief. After an entire afternoon interviewing Dita, the enthusiastic designer for an Amsterdam sex toy company, I really needed some self-indulgent time of my own. Instead, I had to get a cab straight to my sister's townhouse in Hampstead Heath, where the entire family would be waiting to begin the Christmas celebrations. I sighed, deep and long.

The last few stragglers in the taxi queue were getting into London's trademark big black cabs, and as the next one pulled up, I calculated that this one was mine. I ran to the nearest door and threw my bags in on the floor, thanking my lucky stars.

"Oh no," I muttered, when the door on the other side sprang open and a briefcase and gift bags not dissimilar to my own were thrown in the cab.

"Oh yes," my challenger said, ducking his head inside, and grinning across the back of the cab at me. Wow, he was sexy. He waggled one eyebrow at me, suggestively. "And I thought we British were supposed to be so good at queuing."

He'd won the argument outright with that remark.

"I'm really sorry. I didn't see you in the queue. I thought everyone had gone."

He glanced at the driver who was watching over his shoulder, waiting for us to sort it out between ourselves, and then he stepped up into the cab, eyeing me as he did so. I couldn't take my eyes off him either; the urgent hunger of a woman in heat beat out a demanding rhythm in the pit of my belly. I watched him unbutton his jacket and spread his long legs across the roomy floor of the cab, taking full advantage of the space. He was well built, with a rich, languorous sensuality in his expression, like a lion on the prowl. He rested one elbow against the seat, angling his body toward me. The look in his eyes was making me hot; he was staring at me with barefaced speculation. I realized that I was standing with my hands still on the frame of the door, one stacked heel inside the cab poised to climb in, my coat was open and flashing him not only a good length of leg, but a bird's-eye view of my cleavage.

"Where are you headed, perhaps we can share?"

"Hampstead Heath," I mumbled. Looking behind the cab, I saw that no other taxis had joined the rank, but a new procession of weary travelers were spilling out of the terminal and headed our way.

"In that case, let's share, it's on my way." He opened his hand towards me in a friendly, beckoning gesture. I didn't have a lot of choice; I was already late.

Besides, it wasn't every day a sexy guy like that offered to share a ride. In fact, it was practically unheard of in the city. I felt like Santa had come early. Perhaps the holiday spirit was mellowing us. Perhaps it was those brandies I'd had on the flight. Perhaps it was that hunger inside me, taking me over, making me throw caution to the wind. Whatever the reason, I took the hand he offered, sliding into the seat next to him with a grateful smile.

"Where to?" the driver asked, shouting over the blaring radio, then nodding as I gave the address. As he pulled away, he shut the window between him and us and turned his radio even louder.

"We obviously distracted him from his boxing match," the man beside me said. I shrugged at his remark, laughing as the cab lurched and flung me into place on the seat next to him. I caught a breath of his aftershave as I dipped in against him, my hip landing against his thigh as I settled into the seat, my body almost in his arms.

"Sorry," I whispered, straightening up.

"Don't apologize, I enjoyed it," he replied, and gave me the most devastating smile. We were alone in the gloomy interior of the cab and he was sending out very inviting signals. The prospect of being trapped in gridlock was suddenly a whole lot more appealing.

The lights from the underground pickup lane flashed by, racing across his face as he smiled over at me. It was going to take a while to get to my destination; and I wasn't in any rush. He was dark and ruggedly good-looking, and he had the most devilish expression in his eyes. His proximity and boldness, together with the solid rumble of the engine vibrating along the floor and up through my body, brought about a new rush of thoughts about physical pleasure.

The cab whisked out of the terminal area, through the Heathrow underpass and into the night. I was just settling down when, on the first roundabout, my gift bag tipped over and I snatched at it as the contents spilled over the floor.

"Let me help," he said, leaning over to pick up the various packages that had rolled out onto the floor of the cab.

"Thanks." I smiled at him. We were millimeters apart, swaying into each other with the rhythm of the cab. He lifted the packages into the bag that I was holding open. His hand brushed against mine, sending a frisson of electricity darting beneath my skin.

"Someone is going to be getting to unwrap lots of goodies," he commented, as he put the packages back into the bag. He wasn't, however, looking at the gifts, he was looking pointedly at my cleavage, and he wasn't attempting to hide the fact.

"Do you always come onto women who try to steal your cabs?"

If he was going to flirt, then I was up for it. It was the little devil that lived in my head; he made me naughty.

"Only if they are very attractive brunettes."

Right backatcha, huh. He had my full attention. Not to mention the fact that I was very flattered by his comment.

"This one isn't wrapped, does that means it's for you?"

I dragged my eyes off his face and looked at the box in his hand. I swallowed hard and stared, in absolute astonishment. I couldn't quite believe it. He was holding a sex toy in his hand—a clit sucker! *Where the hell had that come from?* I realized that Dita must have slipped it into my bag as I was leaving the design studio in Amsterdam. What should I say, deny knowledge of it and look like a furtive, gauche idiot, or brazen it out as nonchalantly as I could? I remembered Dita grinning at me as she waved me off, and I knew what a woman like Dita would have done.

"A girl has to treat herself sometimes, you know." I managed to get the words out, and then went to grab the box off him, hoping that he wouldn't spot me blushing in the gloomy interior of the cab.

"Oh no," he said, moving his hand out of my reach. "I've never seen one of these before, and you obviously know what it's all about, so why don't you give this poor innocent guy here a demo?"

"A demo," I repeated, aghast. He didn't look innocent at all; he knew exactly what he was doing.

"Yes, you know, show me how it works, I'm fascinated."

He was serious. He offered me the box. A deep pang of longing made itself known between my thighs. I'd been wired all day, watching Dita handle the demo models with such expertise; describing the pleasures they would give. My attention had been rapt. I hadn't even bothered to make notes for my feature; every word and image was emblazoned on my mind. And now there was a provocative man beside me suggesting that I show him what it was all about. My body was on fire with arousal.

I remembered what Dita had said about the toy. I could demo it just as she had, couldn't I? It was the little devil that lived in my head again, urging me to be naughty.

I took the box and peeled off the plastic wrapper. I tried to look as if I knew what I was doing, remembering each move Dita had made. The cab suddenly lurched around a corner as I opened the lid, and the contents slid out onto my lap. I looked down at the cylinder and its pump head attachment. My hands didn't feel altogether steady. Could I really pull it off?

"Wow," he commented. "This all looks very technical."

"Yes, willing mouths are much simpler." *Oh no*! The words were out before I'd even thought it through. His eyebrows lifted, his expression very amused. "I mean?"

"You don't need to explain. I understand you perfectly, and I agree. But let's not spoil the unwrapping of your present."

I was overwhelmed with a heady cocktail of arousal and self-awareness, and I don't know if that remark helped or made things worse for me. But I was determined. I wanted him to know I was a sophisticated, independent woman, not a blushing idiot. I grasped at the plastic covering on the suction pump head and pulled it off, revealing the clit sucker in all its pink-jelly-rubber glory. Before he could say another word, I picked up the cylinder and screwed the pieces together. I switched it on, held it up, and then-and only then-dared to look back at him. The clit sucker made an insinuating purring sound between us, its movement subtle but just visible under the passing streetlights. And now it was his attention that was rapt, just as mine had been when I'd first seen it.

He looked back at me, quizzically.

"There you go. Once it makes contact, it creates a seal. The suction rate is variable," I demonstrated, notching it up and back down, "so you can go for fast pleasure or, draw it out for as long as you can stand it." I felt like I was telling this guy my inner most secrets and desires, somehow, and yet I wasn't. This was me being brave; this was me daring to be as brave as Dita. Maybe it was the way he looked at me. His eyes were burning with keen intensity. Maybe it was the fact I was horny as fuck, and I had a willing man and a fascinating gadget at hand.

"I take it this means you're single?"

"What?" *How did he know that?*

"If you bought yourself the toy?" He gave a suggestive smile.

He was fishing for information. "Oh, right, yes actually." I nodded.

He reached over and traced one hand down my neck, touching the surface of my skin ever so lightly. It

186

was like slow, delicious torture, and yet I felt that he knew exactly what effect it was having on me.

"And you look like you're more than ready to try your new toy; I can see that you're very aroused." His hand dropped down and he ran his fingertips across my breasts, where my nipples stood out under my soft cashmere shirt.

"Yes, I am." I blurted it out, unable to stop myself. But it felt so good to say it aloud. I bit my bottom lip, to stop myself from whimpering loudly as well. "This is quite an arousing situation we find ourselves in, is it not?" It was my turn to fix him with a question gaze. He nodded. He was looking so damned interested. That sent my breathing right out of whack.

"In that case?" He leaned forward and planted a kiss right in my cleavage. The subtle but direct touch sent a hot flare of desire soaring through me. "Why not give me the full, X-rated demo," he whispered, raising his head. "I can see that you want to. It is Christmas, after all." The humidity level between my thighs hit the top of the scale. In that moment I was convinced I'd die if I didn't get some action. Could I really do it? Yes, my body roared. I felt his hand stroke up and over my thigh, easing under the hem of my short skirt with purpose. He groaned in approval when he exposed my stocking tops.

"What about the driver?" I asked, wondering if it would even be possible for me to stop following where this was headed; I was so fuelled up.

"He's far too interested in the boxing to notice what we're up to."

I nodded.

"Just tell me to stop, and I will," he whispered, as his fingers scratched over the scrap of sheer lace panties between him and my lusting sex. He nodded his head at the clit sucker, which I still held aloft in one hand.

"It needs lubricant," I mumbled and then watched in awe as he took the gadget off me, dipped his head toward the pink head, and ran his tongue back and forth inside it, right where it was perfectly shaped to fit snugly over the clit. That sight was enough to drive any woman wild! Before I knew what I was doing, I was moving my hips, rubbing my pussy against his hand. I took the clit sucker back from him and hit the switch, indicating it was all stations go. My coat fell down off my shoulders and my legs moved apart, automatically. He eased my skirt right up and my panties down to my knees.

"Show me," he whispered, leaning over my sprawled hips.

Somehow my hands went into autopilot and I moved the clit sucker into position, the fingers of my free hand opening me up, sliding down either side of my swollen clit.

When I felt the first tug of the sucker on my sensitive, aroused flesh, I nearly lifted off the seat. The contact was so specific; it sent wild torrents of pleasure roaring through me. My back arched, my body leeched to the breathtaking sensations. This little beauty was going to give orgasm on demand! Glancing down, I saw that the man was watching me, fascinated, his hand stroking my thigh soothingly. I was so turned on by him, by the situation-I was about to come at any moment.

"That looks so good," I heard him murmur. I opened my legs wider, and watched as his hand moved closer to my heat.

Where had this exhibitionist streak come from? Was I really doing this, masturbating in front of a complete stranger in a cab? Yes, I was, and it felt thoroughly debauched, dirty and yet so right! Even as the thought crossed my mind, I felt his finger slide inside me, stroking against the hot, slippery surface of my sex, hard and inquisitive. And then it was too much and I was bucking and whimpering, my clit thrumming and my sex clenching as a hot tide of release washed over me.

When I surfaced, I could hear my own raspy breathing, the sound of the engine in the background and a very distant boxing commentary. He kissed my mouth then, and I melted all over again.

"We're almost there," he said, as he turned from me and peered through the fogged window.

"But, I..." I tried to focus, my eyes on the very attractive bulge at his groin. We were almost there, and I had wanted to repay his favor. I wanted to give him head, right there and then.

His eyes were darting and suggestive. "I'll be thinking about how hot you looked just now all night long, when I'm alone in my bed." Yes, I understood that, and I was glad, and I pictured him with his hand on his cock. Oh yes, I wanted to see that. "Would you like to do this again?" he added.

"What, attempt to steal your cab?" I replied, mischievously, as I hurriedly pulled my clothes into place. I snatched the clit sucker off the seat and shoved it into my coat pocket.

"I prefer to think of it as sharing a very pleasurable *ride*, don't you?" He reached into his inner jacket pocket and handed me a business card. His name was Max, Max Lane. And I wanted him. He had touched me, but so fleetingly. I wanted heavy action, bodies rolling together and furious, sweaty, full on, pumping 'n' grinding sex. But it's only Christmas Eve, my little devil reminded me. Yes, I agreed, the holiday season was only just beginning. There was plenty of time for more fun and games.

I nodded, smiling at the card, then slid it into my coat pocket alongside the clit sucker. "And I would like to do it again, Mr. Max Lane? I like to get out of the house by myself for a while on Christmas day, do you?"

"That does sound good." We exchanged looks over the agreement, both of us smiling. "I saw you running

189

over and I couldn't believe it when you got into my cab. I'd been expecting another uneventful family Christmas at my sister's place."

"Me, too," I said and pulled him in for another kiss. His mouth was gorgeous, sensitive and aware. I wanted more of it.

The noise of the driver's window sliding open and a renewed sports commentary on full volume interrupted us. We had arrived. I pulled away and grabbed my bags, jumping out of the cab.

"I'll take care of the fare," Max said, when I opened my bag for cash.

"In that case, I'll pay the next time we share a ride."

I was light headed, dizzy with pleasure. Something about him had made me feel extraordinarily uninhibited and mischievous, and the mood wasn't fading. I was just about to suggest a rendezvous time for the next day when a loud cough drew us back from our mutual reverie.

"Normally I'd charge extra for a Christmas Eve pickup," the taxi driver announced, deadpan. "But I guess I'll have to give you two a discount, on account of the show."

My mouth dropped open.

Max chuckled, breaking the sudden rush of embarrassment I felt. What the hell, it was too late to worry about it now. Max pulled the door closed after me, then rolled down the window. "Call me soon," he shouted, as the taxi pulled away.

"Tomorrow!" I answered, waving, and I realized I hadn't even told him my name. The taxi disappeared into two bright dots on the dark horizon, and I noticed that the rain had stopped. Turning away, I could see the Christmas lights in my sister's window and figures moving inside the house. The muted sound of the Christmas hit parade emerged from the house. I felt a whole lot more ready for

190

this. Ready for this evening, and whatever other magic gifts the season brought for me to unwrap.

SASKIA WALKER

CAUGHT WATCHING

I nearly didn't go to the New Year's party. The seasonal celebrations had been rocking on for two weeks already, with office parties, family and friends to see. I was ready to sidestep this one. Then I reminded myself that my New Year's resolution was to see and do even more. Besides, Natalie insisted I had to go and meet her latest playmate.

Natalie and I worked for the same London media corporation and her roller-coaster romantic life never failed to capture the attention of her friends. She loved that attention. I didn't quiz her about the new playmate over the phone. Part of the fun was finding out whether the playmate was a playgirl, or a playboy.

"Okay, I'll be there." I glanced at my wardrobe dubiously. The party season had severely depleted it, but I managed to find my leather mini skirt and a crop top amongst the pile of abandoned party gear.

The event was being held at a music studio in Camden, and the party was in full swing by the time I got there, the lobby a crush of guests high on seasonal goodwill. A Christmas tree blinked lights in one corner, the framed photographs and discs on the walls were adorned with decorations. Natalie rushed through the crowd when she spotted me, all tumbling dark hair and luscious curves in a PVC bodice and skirt. Around her neck she wore a froth of silver tinsel, boa-like. She hugged me and led me into the main room, where people were dancing. She grabbed me a glass of wine and then took me over to a lean punk with a crown of bleached hair.

"This is Idol," she announced. "Well, that's the name she goes by and I think it suits her, don't you?"

It did suit her. The woman's combination of power and wariness made her both distant and desirable. I nodded and smiled, eyeing her body, perfectly outlined in a simple white T-shirt and jeans. Heavy work boots completed her look.

"Don't ask her real name," Natalie added. "She won't tell anyone, not even me."

Idol draped herself against Natalie, possessively. She gave me a wicked smile and then drew Natalie away onto the crowded dance floor. Natalie wrapped her tinsel boa around Idol's neck, shimmying it as they danced. That was cute. And sexy. Natalie waved and winked at me. She was simmering, visibly. I watched Idol's hand moving around Natalie's hips and smiled back, inspired by their flagrant sexuality.

I drank my wine and edged round the party, chatting with people I knew from the office. When I remembered to check my lipstick, I couldn't find any obvious signs to the bathroom. Gloomy corridors and storerooms branched off from the studios in all directions. I investigated cautiously, the noise of the party receding as a door closed behind me. At the end of the corridor an oblong of light drew my attention. As I got closer, I heard laughter.

"No, I want to wear it." It sounded like Natalie.

I paused when I could see into the room. It wasn't the ladies' at all, it was an office, and the two inhabitants obviously weren't expecting company. Idol was sitting on a high-backed chair, entirely naked. Natalie was standing in front of her, holding a strap-on cock in one hand.

I stepped back, hiding in the darkness.

Idol smiled up at Natalie and put down her wine glass. Lifting her legs she hung them over the arms of the chair. In that one swift move, she exposed the thatch of fair hair over her pubic bone and the glistening slit beneath. She ran one finger over her clit.

194

I glanced back down the passageway. Could I risk going back, or would they hear me? I realized I had inadvertently become a spectator to a private show. And now Natalie had unzipped her skirt and was stepping out of it.

She was wearing high-heeled boots, stockings and garters, no panties. The pale globes of her arse contrasted starkly with the black garters and stockings. The abandoned tinsel boa trailed on the floor, somewhere nearby people were singing Christmas songs in drunken, laughter-filled voices. It was like some debauched Christmas card vision of sex and celebration. I couldn't look away; the scene transfixed me.

Natalie bent over, the strap-on hanging loosely in one hand, like a loaded gun. She tongued Idol's clit, and Idol was wired. "Put it on," she demanded, impatiently.

Natalie climbed into the strap-on, pulling the holster tight against her pussy and between her arse cheeks. She knelt down, one hand on the rigid cock, the other cupping one of Idol's pert breasts. She captured the swollen nipple between her thumb and forefinger, her mouth on the other nipple, sucking heavily.

Idol's head began to roll from side to side against the back of the chair. "Hurry," she pleaded. Natalie began to ease the head of the cock into her slippery hole, spreading Idol's juices over it as she went. "Oh god," Idol moaned. "It's huge."

Natalie chuckled. "I know, but you're going to have to take it, honey." She worked her hips slowly, edging it deeper inside, her hands going to the arms of the chair to brace herself.

Idol began to rock, her eyes wide. "Fuck, it's right there," she whimpered, her hips moving.

My breathing tripped.

I'd heard a sound behind me.

Before I had time to turn around, an arm grabbed me around the waist and a hand fell over my mouth. My heart missed a beat. I was hauled back against a body that enveloped mine.

"Well, well, what have we here, a naughty little voyeur?" The question was breathed low against my ear, followed by a dark chuckle. I reacted, my fingers pulling at the hand over my mouth. The man seized me tighter still, drawing me back and deeper into the shadows, a warning note in his voice. "Stay quiet. You wouldn't want to interrupt them would you, not when she is so close to coming?"

Even if I could speak, what could I say?

I shook my head. After a moment, the hand slipped away from my mouth. I breathed deeply, glancing back. In the gloom, I saw a flash of high cheekbones and hooded eyes, watchful and sparkling with humor. My face flamed at the idea of being caught watching by this man, this stranger. A rather attractive stranger, I noticed. He put one finger to his lips and then pointed me back toward the scene. I obeyed, my attention torn between the women and the dominating presence of the man standing so close behind me.

"Stay quiet..."

I started, but smiled, when his hands found their way around me. The scent of his musk, like warm nectar, seduced me. While he watched over my shoulder, he ran his fingers against my throat, the other hand drawing my body tight against his. He caressed the outline of my breasts through my top. I fought the urge to moan aloud. His fingers tightening on my nipples wired them into the heat between my thighs, creating a molten loop of tension through my body.

In front of us, Idol began to groan, loudly. Her hips plunged on the glistening cock.

I was on fire with arousal. I thrust my hips back against him. He was rock hard. His hands moved to my skirt, shifting the leather on my hips. A pang of deviance deep in my core roared its approval. Yes, I wanted him to lift my skirt, to touch me. I reached down and shimmied the leather up.

He reacted-turned me in his arms, backing me to the wall, his fingers pressing my G-string into my damp slit. He bent to kiss me, his mouth opening me up, making me melt. I lifted one leg along his flank, letting him in. His hips ground against my pussy, lifting me bodily. Hot need welled inside me, my clit sparking.

"You're on fire," he whispered against my lips.

I was. "Do it. Quickly," I urged.

I heard his fly, the rasp of a condom wrapper. Pushing my g-string aside, he lifted me, his hands warm and sure on my buttocks. Easing me down, I was filled-inch-by-inch-with hot, hard cock.

He began to grind, shallow moves, deep inside. I was powerless to do anything but clutch at his shoulders and ride it out, sensation exploding through me each time he hit home. I reached down to feel his girth where we were joined, and he groaned. I rubbed my clit with the heel of my hand, my fingers crooked around the base of his cock. He inhaled sharply, his cock pounding inside me. I was about to explode. Over his shoulder I saw Idol grasp feebly at Natalie's arms, where they were braced on the chair. Her hips bucked wildly, out of control.

I was right there and he knew it. He rammed up inside me. I closed my eyes, crushed my clit and bit my lip, hot spasms rolling out from my core. His cock jerked inside me, making me shudder, boneless with pleasure.

As the heat ebbed away, I realized Idol was getting dressed. We had split seconds before we were discovered.

He noticed too. "I want to see that deviant look in your eyes under brighter lights," he whispered, and nodded towards the party. He lowered me to the floor, raising an eyebrow suggestively.

I nodded, smiling, following him.

Well, my New Year's resolution had been to see and do even more, hadn't it?

SASKIA WALKER

WINTER HEAT

I look out into the drifting snow, and I think about how it stays with you-the good sex. Like echoes of the orgasm, the physical memory haunts the body. The snow today has brought with it the physical memory of the first time a man touched me, the first time a man made me come. Even now, all these years later, the memory grows tangible inside me, proving that the pleasure lasted so much longer than the moment. I sense myself growing damp as I remember every deviant thrill-every tantalizing moment and breathless discovery-as if it were yesterday.

The snow swirled around my legs as I left work that night. I was eighteen, and the icy air cut through my too-thin coat, freezing my stockings to my legs as I made my way out of the warehouse to the bus stop. My knee-high boots were coated in snow by the time I turned the corner onto the street. When I took a deep breath, the sharp cold air traveled into my lungs, quickening my senses. My heart sank when I realized I'd missed the bus.

I was stamping my feet to keep them warm when I saw a figure emerging from one of the factories further along the road. The man made a stark, dramatic outline against the white snow, smoking a cigarette as he made his way toward the bus stop. I watched him with curiosity. The way he looked attracted me instantly. He wore a leather biker's jacket-collar up against the elements-his hair pushed back over his head. Under the jacket, a white shirt and a narrow tie looked out of place on him. When he stopped alongside me, I realized I hadn't seen him around there before. He was built large but lean, his face characterized by prominent cheekbones, and wily, searching eyes.

He flicked his cigarette stub into the snow and smiled when he caught my stare. I couldn't help myself. His bad-boy looks grabbed my imagination in a flash. At night, alone in my single bed in the dark, images of men like him filled my mind while I touched and stroked myself to climax. I dreamed of being taken roughly, being dirty and passionate with a man who knew how to play my body, and did it with no shame.

Watching him from under lowered eyelids, I fast forgot the cold. Forgot everything, except the lure of his bad-boy looks on that cold night. I smiled over at him. "We missed the bus," I remember saying, hoping that he would talk.

He nodded, one finger latched over the knot in his tie as he loosened it, the smile lingering on his face as his eyes roved my body. "You're cold."

It was a statement more than a question, but I answered him, wanting him to talk to me some more. "Yes, aren't you?"

He shrugged. The hard man. His hair shone blue black in the streetlight, and I wanted to touch it. I found myself turning toward him, flirting even. "Do you work around here? I haven't seen you before."

"I came for an interview at Philpotts." He nodded back at the building he'd come from. His accent was South London. It made me smile. It made me feel warm inside.

Then he surprised me. He reached over to my face and stroked a clinging snowflake from my cheek. His touch sent a shiver through me, but this one was no cold shiver. He seemed to be aware of it and a sizzle passed between us, as real as a charge of electricity. "How long until the next bus?"

"About half an hour," I said, rubbing my gloved hands together.

He lifted my hands in his; tugging off the gloves my mother had knitted, tucking them into my pockets before warming my hands inside his larger ones. The act was so strangely intimate, like something a lover would do. No man had ever touched me that way, especially not a stranger. Inside, something essentially female and desirous blossomed, and then quickly turned to liquid heat.

He put his head on one side, looking at me quizzically. "Do you want to go somewhere, to get warm?"

My heart thudded in response to the suggestion. I knew I probably shouldn't go anywhere with him, but curiosity and desire had a strong a grip on me.

He nodded again at Philpotts. "I know a place."

Between my thighs the most intimate part of me clenched. I rubbed my thighs together in response, but then pulled my hands away from his instinctively, unsure. Conflicting emotion ran in my blood. My fingers moved over the buttons on my coat, the same way that my hand closed over my pussy in my bed at night, dreaming of being taken in a man's arms, dreaming of having a man's hand right where mine strayed.

"It's good," he added. "You'll like it."

I nodded.

He took my hand, leading me. Curiosity, fear and arousal assaulted my nerves as I lurched after him through the snow. His hand was large and solid, uncompromising as it enclosed mine. As we walked, I noticed how the falling snow muted the street lamps, making the place seem hushed. It felt as if we were entirely alone. What was I doing? The only thing I knew for sure was that I wanted to follow where he led and have him make me warm.

He went as far as the Philpott building and then turned down the side of it. A security light on the corner of the building cast light in either direction. Beyond that fall of light, where he was headed, it was gloomy and the snow drifted up against the wall. I paused, drawing him to a halt, too, my hand pulling free of his.

"It's all right," he said, eyes twinkling when the light caught them. "There's a warm place here."

"I don't see it," I replied, still unsure.

"What's the matter? Don't you trust me?" He gave a wry smile, like he knew what I was thinking, but beckoned anyway.

Cautiously, I followed at a distance, until I saw him point over at the wall of the building. A large chimneystack jutted out from the brick wall, and the snow was melting away around the area, both on the nearby ground, and on the wall itself.

He moved over to the wall and put one hand against it. "You can warm yourself here. The furnace is inside, at the back of this wall."

Looking up, I saw smoke curling up from the stack, like steam in the sky. Further along the wall, snow still clung. Not there, not where the bricks were warm. He'd been serious, there really was somewhere warm here.

He hadn't meant?

I gave a soft chuckle when I stepped over and joined him against the wall. "Oh, that's good," I whispered when I felt the subtle warmth against the back of my frozen calf muscles. "I thought you meant something else," I added, before I thought through what I was saying.

His mouth lifted and he cocked his head on one side. "Something else?" He put one elbow up against the wall and shuffled closer, until our bodies pressed alongside each other. "You thought I meant come down here for something else?"

His smile was wickedly suggestive, and I gave an embarrassed laugh, realizing what I'd revealed. But then he moved closer, growing serious, his hand stroking along my jaw to lift my face with one finger under my chin. "What something else where you thinking of, Missy?"

My feet shuffled nervously in the snow, my back shifting up against the wall. I glanced away from his stare-then back, compelled to look at him, even though I couldn't bring myself to reply to his question. He gave a dark chuckle, eyes on my lips, strong hand still holding my jaw. He bent and brushed his mouth over mine, barely, tantalizingly, making my lips hum with sensation. Breathless, I stared at him.

"I think maybe you meant this kind of getting warm," he breathed, the back of his hand sliding down the surface of my throat.

A moan escaped me. Raw need roved my body, my nerve endings on high alert. When I didn't resist, his hand stole inside my coat, until it rested around the curve of my breast within my soft, knitted sweater.

Part of me wanted to run, and yet part of me wanted to clutch at his coat and pull him nearer. My hands went flat against the rough bricks to stop myself snatching at him. My lust was like a caged creature, unsure about the open door being offered, and yet longing to find its freedom. But he was older, braver, and he knew what I wanted-what I needed, what I dreamed of alone in my bed at night.

His thumb stroked over the outline of my nipple through my sweater and bra. "Oh yes, this is what you wanted, isn't it?"

In his eyes, an accusing stare.

I nodded, my breast aching for more contact.

"Say it," he insisted.

I wriggled against the wall, pushing my breast into his hand. "Yes," I blurted.

His hand explored me, sure and firm, squeezing the whole of my breast in his palm before moving down the outline of my waist and hip, until his fingertips reached the hem of my skirt. "You wanted a quick tumble to get your blood pumping, you bad girl."

The way he said "bad girl" made my stomach flip. Yes, I was being bad; I was being bad with him. I gasped aloud, inhaling deeply. He smelt of cheap cologne and cigarettes. He likely did this all the time, a quickie with a girl out back, but this time it was me, and I was fiercely glad of it. His touch through my stockings was almost painful on the frozen skin of my thighs. Each stroke he made with his hand was echoed by a pang of need in my pussy. My breath was already coming in quick pants. I reached for him, my hands trembling, eager yet jittery.

He paused when he reached the top of my stocking, roving back and forth across it, moving around its edge to the clasp on my garter belt, plucking at it, his hand nudging up under my skirt. When I moaned against his face, he put his hand under the belt, spreading it around my thigh.

Inside his biker jacket I could feel the lean outline of his torso beneath the crisp white shirt he wore. My fingers stole under the tie and between two buttons, desperate to touch his skin.

His hand curved around the mound of my pussy through my cotton underwear, and it seemed to be the perfect size to hold me there-hold me firm. I whimpered and pressed myself into the precious cup of his willing hand. His eyes narrowed in response, and I could tell he was aroused, too, his body taut against mine. "Getting warmer now?" He sounded amused.

Heat flared in my face, and I nodded. My breath felt trapped in my throat, every cold intake a vivid contrast to the heat inside. When his middle finger moved, pressing the soft fabric of my underwear into my damp niche, my legs felt weak and my head dropped back against the wall, hair catching on its rough surface.

"You're very hot in here," he said, with an accusing chuckle.

I was unable to answer, because my body was moving, responding to the stimulation he was giving me. I was rising and falling in his hand, and each time I did, pleasure shot from my clit, right through my groin. "You made me hot," I blurted suddenly, blushing when I heard my own voice, yet silently begging him for more-for release.

He knew what I wanted. He looked into my eyes as he pushed his hand into my underwear and touched me there.

"Oh, oh," I whimpered. I felt pinned by his stare, opened up by his fingers, my intimate folds tingling with sensation as he explored them.

He was bold, his finger sliding over my dampness, teasing my inflamed clit as he stroked the length of my slit, over, and over again, until my back was moving against the wall, one foot lifted from the ground, my inner thigh against the outside of his.

My hand brushed over his belt buckle, lower, to the bulky shape beneath his fly. He made a sound like a growl in his throat when my hand moved over his erection, his eyes closing for a moment. Then he acted on it and undid the top buttons on his fly, inviting me in, a sly grin on his face.

Could I touch him? I pushed back my tumbling hair with one shaking hand, scared, but acting on instinct. I slid my palm around the head of his cock, marveling at how hot it was, then moved lower, tightening on the shaft as I moved my hand up and down, exploring it under the cover of his dangling shirt tails. Its rigidity and smoothness startled me, starting a new wave of lust, making my pussy clench and my back undulate.

"That's good," he growled under his breath. "Oh yeah, you're going to make me come." He reached lower, stroked a damp smear of my juices up to my clit and centered his fingertip there, rolling over it, back and forth, quick but gentle, almost teasing. And my hand stroked the hot shaft of his cock up and down in response, up and down, until he got even harder, and I saw him grit his teeth and lift his chin.

The heat was building inside me, fast, and the oncoming climax felt heavy and powerful. I wondered vaguely at the back of my mind if my legs would buckle. I heard myself let out a mewling sound, almost lost to the moment. At my back, the heat coming through the wall was like an echo of the startling, raw fire he'd unleashed, between my legs, a climax closing like none I'd ever given myself-all-encompassing, hot and wild. It made me tremble from top to tail, grunts of acknowledgement escaping my lips as he stared into my eyes, urging me on, and as I burned and spilled in his hand, his cock lurched in mine and he spurted against the tails of his crisp, white interview shirt.

He moved closer as he did up his fly, letting my skirt drop. He pressed fully against me, nestling into the spoon of my hips, closing our shared heat in between us, savoring it. I don't remember how long it was, but we were still breathing fast and huddled together, kissing, touching, exploring, when I heard the distant sound of wheels through the snow and saw the headlights lighting up the street. "The bus," I said, "hurry."

We straightened our clothes and ran, out into the street, arms waving, the pair of us falling onto the bus, laughing, glad of it and of each other. And then in the crowded vehicle we grew quiet and smiled across at each other as I attempted to tidy my hair and put my gloves back on, sharing the silent secret of what we had done together back there by the furnace. His stop came first, and he waved and winked at me as he left the bus. After he'd gone, my secret smile stayed with me, as did the physical memory, that first time becoming an essential part of my female self.

I never saw him again. I figured he never got the job that he was being interviewed for. I wondered often enough about what the job was, something to do with the furnace? How else would he have known? Whenever anyone I knew came out of the Philpotts factory I quizzed them at the bus stop. But no one seemed to know him.

How could they not remember him?

I never forgot.

I didn't even know his name, but somehow that didn't matter. For months following that night I would touch myself at night and think only of him as I fell asleep. Often, I'd wake in a sweat, my clit throbbing after dreaming of his body naked and hard between my thighs, just as his clever fingers had been that night, as if in haunting my body he gave me the key to a vast chamber of fantasy, my passion liberated from that moment on.

And now, years later, I'm a successful businesswoman, and a mother, powerful in my own right, but that essential foundation of my liberated female self is still treasured. The physical memory never fails to warm me all over again. I can picture his smile; feel his touch-the bad boy in the virgin snow, the first man to make me come. It taught me to expect the unexpected in life. It taught me that passion can be found and shared in the most unusual of places, and that the memory of a captured moment of pure, shared passion between two people can last a lifetime.

*

CREDITS

Room With a View originally appeared in CAUGHT LOOKING -EROTIC TALES OF VOYEURS AND EXHIBITIONISTS edited by Alison Tyler and Rachel Kramer Bussel, Cleis Press.

Watching Lois Perform originally appeared in SLAVE TO LOVE edited by Alison Tyler, Cleis Press, and THE MAMMOTH BOOK OF BEST NEW EROTICA 7 edited by Maxim Jakubowsi, Robinson Publishing.

Sign Your Name originally appeared in K IS FOR KINKY edited by Alison Tyler, Cleis Press.

Richard's Secret originally appeared in TABOO: FORBIDDEN FANTASIES FOR COUPLES edited by Violet Blue, Cleis, Press, and THE MAMMOTH BOOK OF BEST NEW EROTICA 5 edited by Maxim Jakubowsi, Carroll and Graf.

Hungry for Love originally appeared in GOT A MINUTE? edited by Alison Tyler, Cleis Press.

The Lunch Break originally appeared in EROTIC INTERLUDES: STOLEN MOMENTS edited by Stacia Seaman and Radclyffe, Bold Strokes Books. Also featured in DO NOT DISTURB-HOTEL SEX STORIES, edited by Rachel Kramer Bussel, Cleis Press.

The importance of Good Networking originally appeared in LUST: EROTIC FANTASIES FOR WOMEN edited by Violet Blue, Cleis Press.

In Perfect Time originally appeared in NAUGHTY SPANKING STORIES FROM A-Z, Vol 2 edited by Rachel Kramer Bussel, Pretty Things Press.

The Woman in His Room originally appeared in GIRLS ON TOP edited by Violet Blue, Cleis Press.

A Hook and a Twist originally appeared in BEST BONDAGE EROTICA 2 edited by Alison Tyler, Cleis Press.

The Upper Hand originally appeared in BEST WOMEN'S EROTICA 2006 edited by Violet Blue, Cleis Press.

Counting the Days originally appeared in HIDE AND SEEK-EROTIC TALES OF VOYEURS AND EXHBITIONISTS edited by Alison Tyler and Rachel Kramer Bussel, Cleis Press. Also featured in OPEN FOR BUSINESS, edited by Alison Tyler, Cleis Press.

The Inner Vixen originally appeared in SHE'S ON TOP: EROTIC STORIES OF FEMALE DOMINANCE AND MALE SUBMISSION edited by Rachel Kramer Bussel, Cleis Press, and THE MAMMOTH BOOK OF BEST NEW EROTICA 8 edited by Maxim Jakubowsi, Running Press.

Live Tonight originally appeared in DIRTY GIRLS edited by Rachel Kramer Bussel, Seal Press, and PENTHOUSE magazine.

The Things That go on at Siesta Time originally appeared in NAUGHTY STORIES FROM A-Z, Vol 3 edited by Alison Tyler, Pretty Things Press. Also featured in E IS FOR EXOTIC edited by Alison Tyler, Cleis Press.

It's Just not Cricket originally appeared in RED HOT EROTICA edited by Alison Tyler, Cleis Press

Harvest Time originally appeared in THREE WAY: EROTIC STORIES edited by Alison Tyler. Cleis Press.

Rapt originally appeared in THE MERRY XXXMAS BOOK OF EROTICA edited by Alison Tyler, Cleis Press.

Caught Watching originally appeared in BUST magazine, and NAUGHTY OR NICE? Christmas Erotica Stories edited by Alison Tyler, Cleis Press.

Winter Heat originally appeared in BEST WOMEN'S EROTICA 2008 edited by Violet Blue, Cleis Press.

ABOUT THE AUTHOR

Saskia Walker is an award-winning British author of erotic fiction. Her short stories and novellas have appeared in over one hundred international anthologies including Best Women's Erotica, The Mammoth Book of Best New Erotica, Secrets, and Wicked Words. Her erotica has also been featured in several international magazines including Cosmo, Penthouse, Bust, and Scarlet. Fascinated with seduction, Saskia loves to explore how and why we get from saying "hello" to sharing our most intimate selves in moments of extreme passion. After writing shorts for several years Saskia moved into novel-length projects. Her erotic single titles include The Burlington Manor Affair, Rampant, Reckless and the Taskill Witches trilogy: The Harlot, The Libertine and The Jezebel. Her novels Double Dare and Rampant both won Passionate Plume awards and her writing has twice been nominated for a RT Book Reviews Reviewers' Choice Award. Nowadays Saskia is happily settled in Yorkshire, in the north of England, with her real-life hero, Mark, and a houseful of stray felines. You can visit her website for more info. www.saskiawalker.co.uk

If you enjoyed **UNLEASHED**, you might also enjoy: **DOUBLE DARE**, an erotic romance novel by Saskia Walker

A truth or dare game…
A mutual desire for erotic discovery…

Investment broker Abigail Douglas has got it all, but Abby —the woman—longs for a secret affair, a playmate who knows nothing about her high-powered business world, and Zac Bordino might just be the man. He's mysterious and sexy—just right for Abby's walk on the wild side—but very soon she finds that she wants more, and his mysterious, evasive nature makes her curious. Is there more to this sexy, entrepreneurial club owner than meets the eye? And why does she suddenly feel as if her every move is being watched?

Zac Bordino is perplexed when he realizes that the woman managing his business investments is the same woman he's having an affair with. She's pretending to be a little nobody out for a good time, and because she's a red hot number he plays along, cautiously observing her to get to the truth. From high-powered offices in London to pulse-pounding nightclubs in Paris, they find an insatiably perfect match in business and in pleasure. But when Zac begins to fall for Abby, he has to decide whether to reveal the secret link between them, or try to win her heart first.

EXCERPT

"Abby, what a pleasant distraction." Zac looked her over with undisguised appraisal.

She smiled. "I thought I'd call over to find out some more details about hiring the venue for an office function." *How blatantly feeble an excuse was that?*

"Did you, indeed?" He gave her an indolent smile. "And this would be on behalf of your employer?"

Abby laughed. "Oh, absolutely."

He put his hand inside her coat and slid it open. His gaze fell to her boots, to the flash of naked thigh between them and the hem of the dress. He lifted his head. His eyes glimmered, their irises crystal azure. "You look as if you are dressed for something entirely different."

"It's the weekend."

"It is, and I don't think you came here to discuss a business function at all, did you?"

She smiled and shook her head. Her heart was pounding.

"Seems like that would be above and beyond the call of even the most hard-working receptionist." There was an insinuating tone to his voice that made her feel edgy with need and unsure. He stepped closer still, resting his hand on her hip, inside the coat. His other hand slipped to the light jersey of her dress where it clung to her shoulder and he lifted it lightly, tugging at her breasts with

213

the movement. Her nipples were hard, and the movement of jersey across the taut surface tightened them again.

"I think we both know what I'm here for." She whispered, her body leaning into his, her lips parted.

He gave a dark chuckle. "I can't wait to see what you're going to say next." He glanced down at her nipples where they broke the smooth surface of the material.

Why did it feel as if he was teasing her? "We're adults aren't we?"

"Yes, we are." He breathed in, appreciatively. "And I can smell how aroused you are, just like I could last night."

His words thrilled her. His face was millimeters from hers. He wanted her too.

"Yes," she whispered, "I am aroused. And so are you." Her lips parted with pleasure, the knowledge of reciprocated desire, and anticipation of the event that could follow.

Capturing her hand, he led her to a door stage left, punched a sequence of numbers into the keypad and pulled her through the doorway. It slammed shut behind them. He backed her up against the wall. Grabbing her wrists, he pinned them above her head, his hips pressed hard against hers.

They kissed, their hungry, open mouths locked together. Barely contained animal lust traveled between them, as palpable as electricity crackling across a stormy night sky.

He pulled her toward a door close by and into the room beyond. He fumbled in his pockets, drew out a ring of keys and locked the door behind them.

She glanced around. A dressing table stood against one wall, mirrors over it and on the wall behind. A sink and clothing rails were fitted to the back wall. It was a dressing room.

Zac dropped the keys loudly on the floor and walked over to where she stood. Music stirred through the walls from the auditorium. It was muted, but its dense throbbing sounds reached Abby at the same time as Zac pulled her body to his. He took her coat off, dropping it to the floor, and ran his hands over her breasts.

She breathed out as the light jersey beneath his hands heightened the sensation of skin reaching for skin.

He kissed her neck, brushing the surface lightly, and breathing along her throat. Sensation flew through her from the place where his lips moved on her bare skin. In one long, slow stroke he bent and moved his hands up, from the top of her boots, under her dress, and around the back of her thighs. His hands traced the line of her g-string, pulling at the skimpy line of material.

She moved her hips, responding to the sounds that reached them through the walls. As a woman's voice flew up in a scream of song, Zac moved his fingers into the humid spot inside her. Her head fell back in ecstasy.

She looked into his eyes and moved her hips on his hand. She was burning up, she was so hot for this.

"What is it that you really want, Abigail Douglas?" It was a whisper.

She couldn't reply, because the contact with him had taken away logical thoughts.

He drew back and looked into her eyes with a curious stare, his hot breath covering her face.

"I want you," she murmured. "I wanted you the moment I saw you."

Available now in print and digital format.

Visit www.saskiawalker.co.uk for more details on Saskia's other works. Thank you for reading!

Printed in Great Britain
by Amazon